MURDER IN FOCUS

The Shepton Rise Murders

D R JOHNSON

Cover design by Creative Covers

ISBN 978-1-0687858-2-5

The Shepton Rise Murders

1

Monday

It's late September and, after a largely disappointing few months, Great Britain has been blessed with an Indian Summer. An hour earlier, the pretty town of Shepton Rise had been bathed in warm sunshine. The setting sun highlighted the honeyed tones of the limestone houses and cast long shadows down the high street. Swallows and house martins had swooped and darted in the sky as they hunted down insects. Another month, and they would be making their long journey back to Africa. Now, it's seven-thirty and getting dark. Countless people look at each other and repeat the same phrase, 'The nights are drawing in', as they remember how, at the same time a few weeks back, they would be pruning their roses, enjoying a drink in the garden at the Red Lion, or going for a stroll along the canal towpath.

At the far end of the High Street, only a few minutes walk away from the shops, sits Ginny Fellows' large, imposing house. The windows and curtains are closed to retain the warmth from a sunny day. It's too early in the season to light fires or put on the central heating. Ginny has a guest; her close friend, Adam Broome, is here for Monday Movie Night.

'So what are we watching this evening?' asked Ginny, setting down a tray with two large glasses of wine and two enormous boxes of popcorn.

'Before I answer you, I'm really interested to know what you thought about last week's movie, "Blow Up",' replied Adam.

'Are you, now? Ever since you started that Open University course in documentary photography, you've become a right old bossy boots!'

'It's your own time you are wasting,' said Adam sternly. Ginny burst out laughing.

'Do you remember how our English teacher, Mr

Ashton, used to say that?'

'I certainly do, and to tell you the truth, I know just how he feels. Come on. I can wait all night.'

'Well, for a start, you can't because when it's my bedtime, I'll be kicking you out of the door. But anyway, what can I say about the film? It captured the mood of the swinging sixties, but I can't say I would have wanted to be part of that world. There was an uncomfortable edge to it. One thing I remember was this: you know in that scene when the band was playing?'

'They were the Yardbirds,'

'Were they? You certainly know your rock bands. Anyway, despite all the pumping blues music, the audience was motionless and impassive. It wasn't until that guitarist smashed up his guitar...'

'That was Jeff Beck,' interrupted Adam.

'It wasn't until then that the crowd went wild, fighting for a bit of broken guitar, and then when the David Hemmings character gets hold of it and goes outside, he throws it away.'

'Yes, there's a lot you can read into an Antonioni film,' replied Adam. 'That element of mystery and disquiet was partly why many critics have voted it the best film about a photographer.'

'And the ending! Well, that was just plain weird. I like a story where all the loose ends are tied up. It certainly wasn't a cosy film! So, will you tell me now? What's next on your list of films featuring photographers? Another one from the 1960s?'

'Nope, this time we are going back to the early 50s and to a director who doesn't leave it up to you to figure out what happens next. It's a Hitchcock film, starring James Stewart, called 'Rear Window'.'

'Hitchcock, eh? So there is murder afoot! I was hoping for a rest from all that!' protested Ginny.

'Oh, I don't think a sleepy little town like Shepton Rise needs to be concerned about murder,' said Adam, with a twinkle in his eye, 'So, take a seat, select a cat if you've got one, and we'll begin.'

As if on cue, Ginny's pet, Tuxie, leapt onto her lap. Nearly two hours of uninterrupted stroking lay ahead. She closed her eyes and began to purr, kneading her paws softly and rhythmically into Ginny's lap as the opening music struck up, the TV screen was filled with a sparkly image of the earth, the Universal Studios logo swung around it, and the opening credits began to roll.

Later, when Adam had returned to his own house on the other side of town, Ginny took a moment to count her blessings. Her life had most decidedly taken a nose dive after her husband, Roger, had died in an accident, prompting her to leave London to look after her ageing parents and relocate her theatrical agency business to her family home. Sadly, after her parents passed away, the downward spiral had continued. Whilst she could carry on with her business, it left her fearing panic attacks whenever she left her home, and gradually, her world drew inwards. However, she had recently renewed her friendship with Adam, and although they were taking their blossoming relationship slowly, she did not take for granted the tremendous support he had been in encouraging her to leave the house. *Of course, if murder hadn't come to town, that may never have happened, but I'm grateful all the same,* she thought. *I had better jot down a few notes on what I thought about Rear Window because he will only ask me next week. He'll be setting me homework next!*

2

Tuesday

Adam stopped his car outside a large, double-fronted, Georgian house.

'Here we are, then, Ginny. Marcus certainly lives in a nice place.' He paused as they watched a tall man dressed in a navy blazer and grey trousers leaving through the garden gate. He climbed into a maroon Jaguar and drove away. Adam pulled into the space the Jaguar had vacated. 'I shan't leave until I see you go in the door. Are you sure you don't want me to pick you up later?'

'No, I'll be fine,' replied Ginny, 'I'll call a taxi. I never have problems when I know I'm going home. It's more the other way around - the fear of the unexpected. That's when I get panic attacks. I've no idea how long I will be. The nurse said Marcus often falls asleep, so I may have to wait a while. It's not fair to keep you hanging around.' Adam debated whether to give her a peck on the cheek, but he paused a moment too long, and the opportunity was gone. With an intake of breath, Ginny reached for the door handle, flashed him a smile, and then she was out of the car and walking briskly up Marcus White's garden path. She gave a little wave in Adam's direction before the door was opened by Jamila, Marcus' nurse.

'Mr White is asleep right now, but I'm sure he will be awake soon. If not, I'll have to rouse him anyway because he will need to take his medication. I'll show you to his room, and then I will make a pot of tea.'

Ginny was pleased that she had a moment to herself, with just the company of the sleeping patient, because it gave her a chance to recover her composure. She hadn't expected the memories to come flooding back. *Oh, it reminds me of my Dad's last days at home before it became too much for me and he had to go into the Nursing Home.* She looked around to distract herself. She wasn't in a bedroom, a hospital bed had been placed in a ground floor room overlooking the garden. *This would once have been a very elegant drawing room; I can just imagine a dapper young man, dressed in white flannels and a Fairisle jumper, entering through the French windows saying, 'Anyone for tennis?' But, before it was a sick room, I can see Marcus was using it as a study.* There was a large mahogany desk at one end, flanked by a matching bureau and an antique cast iron safe, on top of which stood a framed picture of a young girl whom Ginny suspected was Marcus White's daughter. On the walls hung framed copies of the Cranthorpe Gazette's front pages. Ginny was just about to have a closer inspection when Jamila returned with a cup of tea.

'I must wake him now,' she said, 'It's time for his medication. He needs his pills four times a day.'

Again, the tableau before Ginny was heart-wrenchingly familiar. On a table to the side of the bed was a plastic container, divided into compartments, each containing an assortment of tablets in different shapes, sizes and colours. Behind it were four large boxes of medicine, and Ginny presumed it would be the job of one of the nurses to apportion the medication for the day, just as she had with her father.

'Do you work out the tablets,' asked Ginny.

'Oh no, there are four of us from the agency. It's already been done when I start my shift.'

By now, Marcus was awake. It had been a long time since Ginny had last visited, but, even so, she was shocked to see how much he had aged. Dark rings circled his eyes. He had always had a fine head of hair, but it was thinning now.

'Ginny!' he cried, 'How good of you to come.'

'I'm only too pleased to see you, Marcus,' she replied, 'I've never forgotten how you used to come and visit Dad. I'll always be grateful.'

'A good man, your Dad.'

'Don't forget to take your medication, Mr White,' scolded Jamila. Marcus held out the hand containing his tablets, shook his head and smiled sadly.

'There was a time when having five a day to keep one healthy was about portions of fruit and veg, but now it means these!' Marcus popped the pills into his mouth, taking a sip of water after each. He coughed and spluttered after the fifth one but managed to keep it down.

'I just can't seem to shake off this flu,' he complained.

'Tell me about the framed newspapers,' said Ginny, trying to shift the conversation away from the old man's failing health.

'Ah! I'm very proud of them. The Gazette has been in my family for six generations, since 1825, and the front page over by the window dates from 1838. Do you see? It's the Coronation edition, and what a fine engraving that is of the young Queen Victoria. We used to employ illustrators in those days, not photographers, of course.'

And so Ginny's visit continued, with Marcus providing a fascinating commentary on the headline news that adorned his walls. What started by stirring unhappy memories about the death of her own parents ended as an enlightening occasion, and Ginny promised that she would return soon. *Strangely, I feel rejuvenated!* she thought.

***

Adam trotted up the steps to the Corn Exchange, or the Corny, as everyone usually referred to it. Once a centre for Victorian trade where merchants and farmers argued and negotiated the price of wheat and barley, it had been a male bastion. Now, it was largely a place of pleasure and entertainment where the citizens of Shepton Rise gathered to stretch and bend in the twice-weekly pilates sessions, click and clack in the knitting club, or shuffle-hop-step in the tap dancing classes that catered for all ages every Saturday.

Ava Nesbitt had invited Adam to come along to a youth group meeting. Ava had been in the same class as Adam's son Robbie at school and worked in the post office. Robbie had told Ava about his father's growing interest in photography, and she had greeted this information enthusiastically.

'Really? Do you think he would come along to the Youth Club? It would be brilliant if he could. I've just learned about a national photography competition we could enter.'

'I'll ask him,' replied Robbie, by now aware of the shuffling and sighing from impatient customers behind him in the Post Office queue, 'I shouldn't think he will take much persuading.'

Adam bounded into the Corny in a failed attempt to look youthful.

'It's fantastic that you could come, Mr Broome,' cried Ava.

'It's a pleasure. Call me Adam.'

'Gather round, everyone,' Ava announced. Gradually the noise in the room descended from the level of an ear-splitting jumbo jet to something that in a factory would still demand the wearing of ear protectors. These excitable youths had been together at school just a few hours earlier. *You would think they hadn't seen each other for years,* thought Adam.

'Shhhh! I don't know if any of you know Adam Broome?' asked Ava.

'I know his son, the copper,' grumbled a boy nicknamed Snakey, 'He caught me scrumping apples and twisted my ear!'

'Anyway, Adam is a photographer,' continued Ava once the laughter died down.

'Oh, I wouldn't say that,' said Adam modestly.

'Adam has agreed to help with a national photography competition that we are going to enter called *My Town.* The beauty of it is that you don't need any special equipment. All the photos have to be taken on a mobile phone. I presume you all have one.' Adam had already read the brief and had come prepared with a bag containing several old phones, as he was worried not everyone would have one. He needn't have bothered as everyone in the room now held up a phone, and he could see they were all superior to his clunky old model! 'And that's not all,' Ava waited for the room to quieten down again as everyone began taking selfies. 'Some of you may have heard of Skye Beattie.' There was a gasp of acknowledgement amongst the girls. One even put her hand up but then hastily lowered it in embarrassment when she remembered she wasn't in school. Most, but not all, of the boys were none the wiser. 'For those that don't know,' Ava explained, 'Skye is a beautiful model who went to school in this area. I was a friend of her older sister, Ocean, and incredibly, Skye has agreed to come back to Shepton Rise for a photo shoot.' There was a squeal of excitement from the girls.

'Don't you know any footballers?' grumbled Snakey, clearly unimpressed.

***

'Hey, guys. I have a favour to ask you,' said Adam, entering the snug - the little room at the back of the pub. He had come directly from the Youth Club meeting to the Red Lion. On Tuesday evenings, the Dead Actors always met here. It was a name they had coined for themselves because they were all actors who had been killed off in long-running TV shows. The Dead Actors were represented by Ginny and had followed her to live in Shepton Rise, attracted by the pretty surroundings and the leisurely pace of life.

Adam told Steve, Doc, Angie and Julia about the photography project, then added:

'So, we've got our top model, but we need some extra people...'

'Moi?' interrupted Steve, pretending to be shocked, 'An actor of my calibre, reduced to a mere extra! I'll have you know I was the leading actor in *City Beat Blue*. I would have thrown you in the slammer for insulting a police officer.'

'You're nicked!' chimed the other three.

'No, please, I didn't mean that,' stammered Adam, 'It's just that we need some ordinary people to…'

'Ordinary!' exploded Julia, but with a glint in her eye, 'Who are you calling ordinary? I was quite the sex symbol in *Stirling Heights* with my black stockings and stiletto heels!'

'You didn't look so pretty after they threw you off that building,' laughed Doc.

'I'm surprised they didn't get her to land on Angie. They could have killed two birds with one stone,' added Steve.

'Birds!' exclaimed Angie in a cockney accent, 'We ain't in a 1960s situation comedy now. Next fing you'll be callin' me a bit of skirt. I ought to give you one.'

'Don't mind if I do, gal,' replied Steve in an accent worthy of Dick Van Dyke in *Mary Poppins*.

'You should be so lucky, I meant bash you on the hooter,' laughed Angie.

Adam was used to the banter between the actors

and often loved to join in, although he wasn't as quick-witted as them. Eventually, he was able to explain that he wanted them to pose as members of the public to be a foil to Skye Beattie.

'You see, some of the kids will want to take realistic documentary-type photos, whereas others will want Skye to pose like she is in a fashion shoot.'

'Listen,' said Doc earnestly, 'I know a little about photography. Let me give you some tips. Now, focus on getting to the bar, zoom in on a round of drinks and see what develops. Just don't be flash with your money!'

'You took so long to tell us what you wanted that my drink has evaporated, so make it snappy,' added Steve.

'Ah, I heard they're all out of crocodile sandwiches,' moaned Angie.

3

Wednesday

Breakfast was ready. Adam knew he could make a good breakfast. Yesterday, it was scrambled egg on toast, but today, it was a full English - two sausages, crispy bacon, a fried egg, fried tomatoes, mushrooms and black pudding. He put the two plates down on the kitchen table and sat down opposite his son, Robbie.

'That looks smashing; you're pulling out all the stops this morning, Dad.'

'You need all your strength, son. Pounding the beat and chasing after criminals.'

'Now I'm a Detective Constable, I don't pound the beat anymore. I get to ride in a car, even if I do have to share it with that bonzo, Cosgrave. How did your meeting at the youth club go, Dad? Did you meet Ava? She's nice, isn't she?'

'I thought you were sweet on Laura?'

'I didn't mean it like that. Anyway, she's married. And before you ask, Laura and I are fine. Just taking things slowly - rather like you and Ginny' Adam coughed with embarrassment and then patted his chest as if he had choked on a mushroom.

'Ahem! Food gone down the wrong way. Actually, it went well, and I'm looking forward to it. Although, I have been upstaged. I'm not the star guest. Ava has invited Skye Beattie, the model, to take part.'

'I've met her.'

'You!' exclaimed Adam, genuinely choking on a mushroom, 'You don't exactly swan around in the world of high fashion.'

'I said I've met her. I don't know her. It was years ago when I was a new recruit. Cosgrave and I got sent over to the newspaper offices because they'd reported a break-in. Skye was doing a work placement there. There was a right old mess in the newsroom. I remember the photographer was really annoyed because thieves had stolen all his negatives and his new digital camera. The computers had been trashed. Senseless! We never did catch the vandals that did it. But yes, Skye was there. I'm not surprised she became a model; she was very pretty. I think she left for London soon afterwards.'

***

Adam took a deep breath and stepped through the entrance door of the Cranthorpe Gazette. He was nervous because he was out of his comfort zone and was worried that he was trying to run before he could walk. *Still, nothing ventured, nothing gained!* He attracted the attention of a woman working at a desk behind the reception window.

'Hello, my name's Adam Broome, I rang yesterday.'

'I remember. I'm awfully sorry, but Mr Steele has had to pop out. He shouldn't be long. You could wait here if you like.' She indicated two chairs in the hallway. Between them was a small table on which was the latest edition of the newspaper, and facing them, a large TV screen tuned to the BBC rolling news channel was showing the weather forecast. 'Or, perhaps you would prefer to wait in the newsroom?'

'Oh, the newsroom, please.'

The woman introduced herself as Lauren and showed Adam into a large open-plan office. Only two people were working in here, both studying computer screens. Many of the desks in the room were piled with newspapers and general clutter.

'It's funny, but I imagined it would be busier,' observed Adam.

'Every desk would have a reporter sitting at it, once upon a time,' commented Lauren wryly, 'But times are tough for local newspapers now and as staff have retired or moved on to other jobs they haven't been replaced. Take a seat.'

Adam looked around the room. One of the two reporters was staring intently at his computer, his eyes only inches from the screen, seemingly oblivious to Adam's arrival. The other, who looked older, was leaning back on his chair and staring into space. Adam immediately noticed the camera sitting on his desk.

'Is that the new Nikon Z9?' This woke the man from his daydream, and he patted his camera, smiled to himself and nodded.

'Sure is. This bad boy has a weather-sealed, magnesium alloy body; I could be in a blizzard or a dust storm, wouldn't touch it!'

Dust storm! We are in Cranthorpe, for heaven's sake, not

the Sahara Desert! 'Very useful,' agreed Adam.

'Oh yeah, it shoots 20 frames per second, so you can bet your bottom dollar that I won't be missing any fast action scenes.'

Hmm. Thought Adam. *Like the Under-Twelves' Sunday football matches.* 'Impressive!' he said aloud.

'The vari-angle touchscreen has 2.1-million dots!'

'More than enough for anyone. Wow!'

'And there are eight stops of IBIS, that's In-Body Image Stabilization, so even in low light with a telephoto lens, I tell you, absolutely zero camera shake. They ain't cheap, but sometimes, if you want results, you've simply got to splash the cash!'

I bet you didn't have to put your hand in your own pocket - the Gazette will have bought it. 'I suppose it has Bluetooth connectivity?'

'Of course it does; what do you take me for? An amateur? Anyway, what do you do?'

'I suppose I'm an amateur photographer,' replied Adam sheepishly.

'Hah!' scoffed the photographer. 'Anyway, I've got work to do,' The man scoffed and turned back to his computer, although Adam noticed that his hands didn't go anywhere near the keyboard. Adam thought he could detect a slight head shake from the other man working in the room, indicating exasperation with his pompous colleague.

'Sorry, I'm late,' boomed a voice. 'I'm Bradley Steele. I was visiting our proprietor, who is rather poorly, and got held up in traffic on the way back from Shepton Rise.' Adam got up to shake the man's hand.

'The roadworks make everyone late,' he sympathised. 'I got stuck in traffic coming the other way.'

'We could fill our newspaper with the complaints that we get about it from the general public. Anyway, come on through to my office,' said Bradley, leading the way, 'I see you've been getting to know Jason. I would be surprised if you got a peep out of Dillon! Would you like a cup of tea? I'm parched.'

'Yes please, I'd love one.'

'Hold fire, I'll go and ask Lauren to make us some.'

It dawned on Adam that he had seen Bradley somewhere before. *It was when I took Ginny to see Marcus White. He was just leaving. But of course, Ginny told me Marcus owned a newspaper! That'll be why Bradley was visiting.* Adam looked around the editor's office. The headquarters of the Gazette were once in an old Victorian building close to the centre of town. That site was now a car park, and the Gazette had moved to a modern industrial estate. However, Marcus had managed to create a feeling of heritage in the way that he had decorated his office, from the red and cream Turkish rug to the brass light fittings and the mahogany furniture. Photographs of previous proprietors and editors were displayed on the walls. Adam was struck by a framed photo of a younger Bradley Steele in an army officer's uniform.

'Despite being in a modern building, this room just oozes history,' said Adam when Bradley returned.

'Oh, yes, we have a long tradition. There are a few older newspapers, like the Stamford Mercury, for instance, but not many publications from the olden days are still in existence.'

'So, you were in the army, then?' said Adam, indicating Bradley's photograph and aware that he was stating the obvious.

'Yes, as a young man. I was injured in combat and invalided out. I went to University and ended up here.'

'It must have been quite a change from soldiering to working on a newspaper,' commented Adam.

'Yes, it was, although there is some overlap. You need to be quick-thinking and react to a turn of events in both professions. When I came out of the army I missed the camaraderie, so when I went to University, I threw myself into the sporting life. Whilst others from my course were spending all their free time in the Student Union bar, I was sculling up and down the river or training on the rugby field.' He paused when Lauren arrived with two mugs of tea. 'So, what can I do for you, Adam?'

'I've come with two hats on, really. Firstly, I want to tell you about a photography project that the Shepton Rise Youth Club will be working on and that I'm going to help with. We are very lucky to have the company of a top London model for a day, Skye Beattie. I believe she was an intern here.'

'Ah yes, I remember her well. Very beautiful but not cut out for working in the backroom. I'm sure we can run a feature in the Gazette.'

'And with my second hat on, I wondered if I could document it for you. I'm a keen photographer, and I would love the opportunity to provide you with some photographs for the newspaper.'

'By all means. I can't promise you the role of exclusive photographer, though. I wouldn't want to put Jason's nose out of joint. I'm sure we'll all want to pop over and see Skye in action. Email me the details. It all sounds very interesting. Just what we need for the paper - a feel-good story for our readers. Not a lot happens around here, as you'll well know. Unless you count road rage caused by those infernal roadworks!'

26

4

Several years ago

It was a risk, but Dillon was in a hurry. He wouldn't normally walk this way home from school, even though it was the shortest route on a map. Usually, he would turn left instead of right and cut down a number of passageways and back streets before arriving at the council estate where he lived. It was a circuitous route, but he would avoid confrontation. Dillon envied the kids from Shepton Rise. They were lucky enough to catch a school bus from Cranthorpe High School and be deposited close to home. Even more fortunate were the children whose parents waited for them outside the school gates and drove them safely to their front door. Dillon was Cranthorpe boy and didn't live far enough away to qualify to travel on a school bus. He lived alone with his mum and she had to work all day. Four years had passed since his mother used to be waiting at the Primary School gates for him. His father was still around in those days. Now, Dillon was what was commonly known as a latchkey kid. Not for him kicking a football around with the neighbourhood kids on the square of green outside his house. Instead, once he was home, he would switch on the TV to provide some background noise and give the illusion that he wasn't alone, and then curl up on the sofa with a book.

It would be different today, though. Dillon's dad was going to be making a rare visit. He would pick him up from home and take him to MacDonalds. It was a pity his father couldn't pick him up from school, but there were always too many parked cars, and his dad couldn't manoeuvre his massive truck around them. So today, Dillon couldn't be late.

He hadn't seen Cosgrave today. He was in the year above Dillon, so at least he didn't have to share a classroom with him, but he always kept well out of his way anyway. Cosgrave lived on the next road to Dillon, and he was the reason that Dillon avoided the direct way home. Cosgrave and his mates were not people you wanted to run into. So today, Dillon made sure that he had everything he needed to take with him already packed in his bag - his homework, his pencil case, and an essay that had just been marked nine out of ten that he wanted to show his mother. Dillon was good at English.

When the bell rang to signal the end of the school day, he was out of his seat like a shot from a cannon. His classmates might have described him as looking like a frightened rabbit. He dashed down the corridor, through the playground and out through the school gates, surprising the caretaker who had only just unlocked it. *Yes,* he thought, *I'm the first one out.* Dillon slowed down to a quick walk. The gang of boys he was trying to avoid didn't like school, but they wouldn't be in such a hurry as he was to leave, so they wouldn't catch him. Instead, they would be swaggering around the playground trying to impress the girls with mock fights, those with skateboards would be attempting tricks using the kerb outside the school.

Dillon had just began to breath normally when suddenly, out of the doorway of the *Eight 'til Late* shop, stepped the figure of a larger boy, blocking his path.

Cosgrave! *Oh no, that's why I haven't seen him today! He must have bunked off school, and now he's waiting to meet his mates.*

'Hello, Titch!' Cosgrave never referred to Dillon by his real name. 'Where are you off to in such a hurry?' Dillon was too embarrassed to tell him he was going to meet his dad. Cosgrave had a mum and a dad at home. Besides, anything that Dillon said would be met with derision, so he kept quiet. 'That bag of yours looks very full. Let me relieve you of that heavy load.' Cosgrave grabbed Dillon's rucksack by one of the straps and yanked it off, sending Dillon spinning to the ground. 'Nah! there's too much in here; you've gotta get rid of some of this stuff!' Cosgrave unzipped the bag and emptied it onto the pavement. Dillon's essay went fluttering away down the street. Cosgrave noticed Dillon's Star Wars pencil case and stooped to pick it up. 'You ever played *Pick Up Sticks?*' he asked, opening it, and he grabbed hold of the contents and threw them high into the air. Pencils and pens bounced and scattered across the road. An eraser disappeared down a drain. Cosgrave laughed and then continued on his way to meet his mates, leaving Dillon scrambling to retrieve his possessions before they were run over by passing traffic.

'Can I help?'

Dillon looked up from his position kneeling on the wet pavement into the blue eyes of a pretty young blonde girl two or three years younger than him. She was someone he thought he had seen before but had never spoken to. Girls didn't figure much in Dillon's life, only in his imagination, and he generally avoided eye contact with them. The girl flashed him a smile, and Dillon noticed that she wore braces on her teeth and had freckles on her cheeks. Without waiting for an answer, she started picking up pencils.

'Hello, My name's Skye.'

***

FIVE YEARS AGO

Bradley Steele was strictly old school. He came from the era when newspapers were created by assembling lines of individual characters, letters and numbers on a typesetting machine. So even now that the Cranthorpe Gazette was fully digital, he insisted that his reporters printed out copy for him to approve.

'That's not bad at all, Dillon,' said Bradley, peering over his wire-rimmed glasses, 'The last paragraph's a bit flowery; you can lose a couple of adjectives - here and here.' Bradley crossed out two words, 'And change this from furious to outraged. And that will be ready to upload.'

'Thanks,' muttered Dillon. The newsroom door opened, and Jason Prince strolled in, his Nikon camera slung over his shoulder.

'Chief,' he said, confidently acknowledging his editor. 'I've got some great pictures. I don't know how you guys did it in the old days, having to wait until you'd developed your film before you knew if you'd had had a good day. I tell you, this lot's the whole package. I'll get them downloaded, and I can put my feet up!'

Jason's self-confidence annoyed Dillon, although he was careful not to let it show. He didn't think it was fair that he received more criticism than Jason. He knew the reason though. Whereas Bradley knew how to write, having started at the Northern Echo before moving on to the Manchester Guardian, he didn't know one end of a camera from another. To Dillon's eye, some of Jason's work lacked grit and dynamism. Maybe that wasn't appropriate for a small-town newspaper, but Dillon felt that the photographer lacked the ambition or talent to become the next Don McCullin or Danny Lyon. It wasn't just the quality of his work that got to Dillon, though. Jason's ease with the opposite sex and ability to banter with the editor made him feel inadequate.

Lauren, the editor's secretary, popped her head around the door.

'Mr Steele. Your visitor has arrived. The intern.'

'Ah, show her in; she may as well start by meeting these two reprobates,' Bradley said cheerfully.

Dillon and Jason looked up without enthusiasm. The last intern had only lasted two weeks. He was a student who couldn't get used to the fact that you had to get out of bed early to catch the news. Dillon's heart skipped a beat. He realised that this time, it would be different.

'Gentlemen,' announced Bradley, 'Let me introduce you to Skye.'

***

Dillon and Skye got on fine, but their relationship hadn't developed in the way that Dillon had hoped it would on that day when she first arrived at the Cranthorpe Gazette. He had never forgotten the time when Skye had helped pick up his scattered pencils, but to his intense disappointment, she had no memory of the event. Looking back, he realised that he hadn't said more than a few words at the time and had never spoken to her since. He had not encountered her on the way home from school again either because he had later noticed her in the queue for the Shepton Rise school bus. She must have been in Cranthorpe for a different reason. He watched her from afar during his remaining years at school. Her hairstyle changed, her braces came off, and her smile grew brighter, but boys his age didn't talk to younger girls. Truth be told, Dillon did not talk to any girls outside the classroom. When he left school and started working for the Gazette he tried not to think about Skye. He imagined it was like a sailor looking back on an encounter with a beautiful siren or a mermaid, no longer able to determine if she had been real.

'Oh, you're so sweet, thank you,' she would say now, or, 'What would I do without you, Dillon?' when he helped her with an assignment or, more often than not, wrote the whole piece for her. He knew she wouldn't stay working for the Gazette for long; her heart wasn't in it. The internship was just a stepping stone. Skye quickly learned that there was very little glamour in working for a local newspaper. Covering stories about townsfolk demanding a bypass or objecting to plans for an out-of-town supermarket would never help her achieve her dreams. She wanted to become a model, a supermodel even. She was certainly pretty enough, and much to Dillon's chagrin, the person she gravitated to, the one who said he could help, was Jason!

Dillon guessed why Skye had jumped at the chance to accompany him on today's assignment. Jason, who she preferred to spend her time chatting and joking with, had been sent to the city to photograph a politician visiting a community graffiti project in an underpass, which was not exactly Skye's cup of tea. However, once she learned that Dillon had an appointment to visit a theatrical agent who had recently moved from London, she rushed in to see the editor to ask if she could tag along. Bradley was only too pleased to agree, as he hadn't yet found a suitable role for her.

Ginny showed Dillon and Skye into the living room. She was extremely unenthusiastic about the appointment, failing to see how an article in a provincial newspaper would benefit her, and had only agreed to do it so as not to disappoint her father. He was upstairs, seriously ill in bed, and had been visited the week before by an old friend from the Rotary Club, Marcus White, who was the proprietor and major shareholder of the Gazette. The whole thing had snowballed from there.

Ginny sighed inwardly. She looked around the room and saw ornaments on every surface that had been there all her life: Delicate porcelain figurines, family photographs in ornamental silver frames, Venetian glass bowls and engraved brass cigarette boxes. Distressingly, they were interspersed with sympathy cards because it had only been a month since her mother had died. Ginny turned her gaze back to the shy, awkward reporter and his pretty young companion and smiled.

'Tell me, Mrs Fellows, what brought you back to Shepton Rise,' asked Dillon.

Oh no! Thought Ginny. *How do I put a positive spin on this? I can't exactly say my husband died in an accident and my parents were both terminally ill, so I came back to look after them.* 'Well, I thought it was time for a new challenge...' *The trouble is, he doesn't make eye contact.*

'How does living in London differ from being in Shepton Rise?'

It's hard to compare because I very rarely ever leave the house. It was the same in London after Roger died. Ginny managed a bright smile. 'Now we are in the age of the internet and emails it doesn't make a lot of difference. Of course, if one of my clients is acting in the West End, it takes a little more effort, but as most of them are on TV, their performances come to me.'

The interview was not a great success. Publishable

but hardly riveting. After it had finished, Ginny was surprised when Skye asked a question. Up to then, she hadn't said a word.

'Mrs Fellows. It's my dream to live in London and become a model. I wondered if you could give me some advice?'

'Not personally. I only represent actors, but I do have a friend who runs a model agency. I'll write her name and number down for you. Tell her Ginny Fellows says, *Hi*.'

5

Thursday

Jay emerged from the shower, leaving clouds of steam and aftershave in his wake. He had knotted a white towel loosely around his waist. He walked over to the floor-to-ceiling window and stretched, causing the dragon tattoo that covered most of his torso to ripple. He watched the activity on the Thames for a moment. Skye's apartment in London's Canary Wharf was in a prime location.

'Hey, babe, where did you say we were going tomorrow?'

'Shepton Rise. It's where I was born,' replied Skye.

'Well, nobody's perfect.'

'Hey you!' Ske laughed, flinging a cushion at him, 'For your information it's a pretty little town, although it's a world away from all this.'

'Say, you ain't been looking happy lately. What's up? It's all been going good. You've got that Vogue shoot coming up, a perfume contract being talked about, and you've got an audition for that Reality TV show next month. It's all cool, babe.'

'I didn't want to bother you, honey. You are always so good to me, but something has come up that might threaten all of that.' Jay furrowed his brow. Anything that was a threat to Skye was a threat to him and his lifestyle.

'You tell me, babe. You know me. I can sort it. Do you remember how I persuaded that paparazzi scum to leave you alone? Luckily for him, he could swim. Pity his camera couldn't. I still smile when I pass that section of The Embankment.' Skye paused momentarily, then reached into her bag. She took out an envelope and extracted a piece of paper, smoothing it out on the glass coffee table.

The message was collaged using letters cut out of a newspaper.

'Two hundred grand, or I will publish the rest of this and the others,' read Jay. 'What is it? What does it mean?' By way of an answer, Skye withdrew a photograph from the envelope. Jay looked down at an image of Skye, taken when she was much younger. She was looking coyly into the camera lens, and shockingly, she was completely naked!.

Jay snatched up the envelope and studied it.

'It's got a postcode,' he growled, 'Shepton Rise. That's where we are going, innit! When did this come?'

'It was a couple of weeks ago. I can't remember the date right now, but it was the day when that politician resigned for telling lies.'

'Right. I'll get to the bottom of this, babe, and put a stop to it. You mark my words. I'll sort it good and proper. I may need a few expenses, though.'

'I'll make it worth your while, honey.'

'Somebody is going to get what's coming to them!'

6

Friday Evening

'The Red Lion was all prepared for a party. As usual, Pete put a lot of effort into choosing a playlist of songs. Tonight there was a modelling theme, and as usual, although they enjoyed the music, hardly any of his customers appreciated his endeavour. As soon as he saw Skye Beattie step through the doors of the pub, Pete selected one of his favourite Kraftwerk songs and the line *She's a model, and she's looking good* reverberated around the room. Skye paused for a moment then beamed in delight. Her partner, whom everyone later learned was called Jay, looked less pleased to be there. Visiting old-fashioned country pubs did not figure largely in his social life, nor was he enthusiastic about the idea of the evening starting at eight o'clock. The nightclubs he frequented didn't get going until after midnight.

Meanwhile, Skye circulated, shaking hands with people she knew and some she didn't. When she reached Ava, she gave her a long, sisterly hug.

Pete changed the track. Apart from the landlord, Skye was the only person who recognised the introduction to the song. First, the strings came in, and then the percussion started, and Skye moved into the centre of the room. When Madonna sang *Strike a Pose,* she re-enacted the original video perfectly and soon nearly all of the girls in the pub were freezing in a dramatic pose. They were voguing!

Roxette's *She's Got the Look* and Duran Duran's *Girls on Film* followed. Then, it was a toss-up as to which was funnier - the sight of Lenny Peters, taking a night off from studying horseracing form and dressed in his usual flat cap and tweed jacket, parading around as the whole pub sang *I'm Too Sexy for my Shirt* or Pete, wearing a Santa beard, legs splayed and playing air guitar to ZZ Top's *Sharp Dressed Man.* Perhaps Lenny had the edge, although some of his moves were decidedly not politically correct.

'Hello,' said Adam, shaking Skye's hand. 'Ava has asked me to work with the youth group on the photography project. It's good of you to come back to Shepton Rise.'

'I've been looking forward to it,' smiled Skye. 'I've caught up with some schoolfriends, and I see some people from the Gazette over there that I must chat to. One person I hoped to meet up with is Ginny Fellows. I don't suppose you know her, do you?'

'I do, actually. She's a good friend of mine. I'm afraid, she isn't here. Ginny isn't a fan of crowds.'

'Oh, that's a shame. I owe it all to her. It was her friend who opened doors for me. I'm still with the same model agency. I'd love to see her again and say thank you.'

'I'll give you her number,' said Adam, 'Ring her. I'm sure she would be happy for you to drop by.'

Skye went over to talk to the newspapermen. The three people she had been in most contact with were here: the editor, Bradley Steele, reporter Dillon Richards and photographer Jason Prince. Skye felt a pang of guilt because she remembered that Dillon had once written to her, but caught up in the whirlwind of her new career, she had never found time to reply to him. Bradley was as charming as ever.

'My dear girl, how good to meet you again. Your progress has not gone unnoticed. Well done!' Dillon still seemed very shy and avoided eye contact, looking over Skye's left shoulder as he offered her a limp handshake. Jason's eyes, meanwhile, seemed to focus on Skye's breasts, and he moved in to kiss her on the cheek. Adam watched this exchange and saw Skye's boyfriend looking on from across the room. Jay was tense, fists clenched and a vein pulsing in his neck. He clearly did not approve of anyone kissing his girlfriend.

Adam noticed Joey approach Jay for a chat. Joey ran the local gym, Fit For Life, and he, like Jay, was a Londoner, spending his early and troublesome years in Brixton. Now, however, Joey was firmly ensconced in the Shepton Rise community. His gym was going from strength to strength. The conversation appeared to be cordial, but there wasn't a lot of warmth. They looked like two prize fighters weighing each other up. After a while Jay broke away and went to the bar to make use of the free tab Pete had set up for him and Skye.

'Yo!' he called to Pete, 'Haven't you got any modern music, man? This stuff's for old codgers.' Pete smiled, although inwardly he bridled.

'It's what we like around here. It stirs the memories.'

Jay made a loud, sucking noise through his teeth, but made no further comment. By way of a response, Pete selected *Coat of Many Colors* by Dolly Parton next. He turned the volume up a notch and was gratified to hear a roar of approval from some of the customers in the pub.

Meanwhile, Skye continued to mingle - smiling, chatting and posing for selfies. When she returned to the bar to top up her glass of Prosecco, only one person noticed her pause and lean towards Jason. Dillon was standing nearby, but not near enough to hear her whisper:

'We have to talk!'

48

7

Saturday

'Hello Ginny.' Ginny would have recognised the voice immediately even if Joey had not been in her phone's address book. His South London accent, peppered with Jamaican inflexions, was not something you heard very often in sleepy Shepton Rise.

'How are you, Joey? Nice to hear from you. I'm afraid I haven't been keeping up with that exercise plan that you devised for me. Did you go to the party at the Red Lion? I didn't quite feel up to it myself.'

'Don't worry, I'm not ringing to ask about your fitness levels. Yes, I was at the party. Adam told me that Skye was going to come and see you. It's why I'm ringing.'

'Oh, really? I'm intrigued.'

'It kind of goes against the grain to tell tales, you know what I mean? Being a snitch - well - it's not part of my background.'

'Oh, you mean when - how did they put it back in the day? When you used to be rude!'

'Ha ha,' laughed Joey heartily, 'Nearly right. We used to be called Rude Boys, but that was a Jamaican expression a little before my time. In my day, we were called Gangsta.'

'Well, it's commendable that you have turned your life around. So, what's worrying you, Joey, prompting a battle with your conscience this morning?'

'It's Skye's boyfriend, Jay. I've never met him before, but you develop an instinct for people. It's a kind of Gangsta radar. I mean, he's got a pretty face and a supermodel girlfriend. He's wearing expensive clothes, you know - the special edition trainers, designer sweatshirt and of course, he's flashing lots of gold jewellery, but I've got this feeling about him, you know. I think he's a bad man and I just wanted to warn you.'

'That's very kind of you to think about me, Joey. I will be most alert.'

***

'Will you get a taxi home again, Ginny?' asked Adam later that morning. 'I can't really hang around, even if you wanted me to, as I need to meet Skye and take her to the photo shoot.'

'Don't worry about me, I'll be fine,' replied Ginny. 'Have fun; it all sounds exhausting and a little too unpredictable for me. I'm looking forward to a nice relaxing chat with Marcus.'

Ginny was pleased to find that Jamila was the nurse on duty again.

'He may still be fast asleep. He had a business meeting with Mr Steele from the newspaper earlier, and he was exhausted by the end of it.'

Marcus was sleeping when they entered his room.

'Don't worry, I'm in no hurry,' said Ginny, walking over to the open French windows. 'It's a glorious day, isn't it? It's good to see that Marcus is getting some fresh air. I'll move my chair over here and sun myself while I wait for him to wake up.'

It was a full hour before Marcus gave a long groan and opened his eyes. He blinked several times, getting used to the sunlight and then smiled when he noticed Ginny. She carried her chair back to his bedside and touched his hand.

'Hello, Marcus. Jamila tells me you are tired out from having meetings. I'm surprised you are still so involved.'

'Oh, it's not so bad. Did I tell you that the newspaper has been in my family for six generations?' Ginny smiled. She remembered her parents used to repeat themselves too. 'Bradley just brought me a few things to sign. Extending the lease and the like. Say, tell me, Ginny, did Bradley remember to shut the safe door? I think I fell asleep before he left.' Ginny jumped up to check.

'Yes, Marcus. It's well and truly closed,' she replied.

'He wasn't my only visitor. The doctor called first thing. He can't understand why these flu-like symptoms are persisting. He's determined that I should go into hospital and be hooked up to a machine so it can monitor me.'

'I suppose it's for the best.'

'Yes. I'm not looking forward to it, though. Bradley said I should insist that I stay at home, but I don't think I will. I suppose they know what they are doing. The doctor booked me in to go tomorrow.'

Ginny's heart fell as she realised the implications of this development.

'Marcus, I may not be able to see you when you go into hospital. Or at least if I visit, I will have to come with my friend, Adam. It's just the kind of place that sets off my panic attacks.'

'Don't you worry about it, my girl. It's important that at least one of us stays healthy. Now, did I tell you about the time that your father and I rode to London on a tandem?...'

***

Adam was in the Recreation ground, talking to Ava.

'I never imagined having a supermodel in town would generate this kind of interest, Ava. I felt like the Pied Piper, coming down the High Street, leading a crowd of onlookers. It was a hard job trying to keep them out of the shots. Even if they weren't directly in the way, I had to make sure they weren't reflected in the shop windows.'

'Some of the kids have shown me their photographs on their phones,' said Ava, 'They look great. They are so lucky to have all that technology in their pockets. I suppose in your day, you had a camera on a tripod and had to get under a black cloth holding up a big flash. Watch the birdie!'

'Ha ha, You cheeky monkey! I'm not that old! Although now we are here at the Rec, I'm looking forward to resting my aged bones while I sit down and enjoy my picnic.'

'So what's the plan?' asked Ava,

'We will have a thirty-minute lunch break, and then we could take some shots of Skye on the play equipment - on top of the slide, on the swings and roundabout and so on. Then, I thought we could celebrate that we are a country town seeing as we have the footpath through the woods starting from here.'

'Good idea,' replied Ava, 'We should have all bases covered then; action shots on the equipment and some nature photos. I've noticed that not all the kids have been that engaged so far.'

'Yeah, Snakey, for instance. I'm not sure if he's taken any photos yet. He's a bit of a loner, that one.'

'Yes, he's prone to wander off. It's good for him to come to the Youth Club, but he often won't join in with group activities. Anyway, I'll go and have a chat with some of the kids. See you later.'

'Hello, Mr Broome, isn't it? You came to the newspaper office.' Adam turned to see the secretary from the Gazette.

'Hi, Lauren. Goodness, this must be a big news story. I think I've seen all of you today. The photographer is here somewhere, although I'm not sure where he is now.'

'You mean Jason,' prompted Lauren.

'Yes, and that quiet reporter was with us too. He seems to have disappeared as well. I can see the Editor, Bradley, though. He's talking to my son over there.'

'He looks familiar, your boy. I'm sure I've seen him before somewhere.'

'You probably have. He's a policeman. He's off-duty today, although now he's a Detective Constable he doesn't wear a uniform any more. But he told me that when he was just an ordinary bobby he came to your offices after you had a break-in.'

'Ah, that will be when I met him. I'm good at remembering faces. His, for instance.' Lauren gestured towards a figure disappearing down the footpath into the woods. 'I perhaps shouldn't say it, but I didn't care for him.'

'That's Skye's boyfriend, Jay,' said Adam, 'I know what you mean. He's a bit full of himself. Where did you meet him?'

'He came to the office and demanded to see the boss, as he called Bradley. Effing and blinding, he was.

Then he stormed into the newsroom.'

'Oh, that must have been an unpleasant experience. By the way, have you closed the newspaper office today?'

'No, I don't work on Saturdays. My colleague, Karen, is in today. Mind you, Bradley forgot that it was my day off earlier. He nearly bit my head off and told me to get back to work. I don't know why he was in such a grumpy mood. I wonder what's been eating him!'

'Well, whatever has been eating him, biting your head off in retaliation seems a bit extreme,' laughed Adam. 'If he's a bit peckish, he should have called in at Heavenly Delights and bought a flapjack. Speaking of which, I bought one as a treat for Skye. I wonder where she's got to.' Adam scanned the recreation ground. Then, seeing townsfolk scattered throughout the Rec, looking happy and relaxed, he decided to capture the moment on video. He pulled out his phone and started filming, revolving slowly on the spot. He saw Steve and Angie competing to see who could swing higher, and Julia and Doc sitting on a picnic blanket eating lunch. Robbie came into view, still talking to Bradley. On the footpath, three girls emerged from the woods. They clustered together, looking at each other's phones and giggling. Adam saw Ava walking away from a group of teenagers and approached her, still recording.

'Have you seen Skye?' he asked. She shook her head. Then a bang echoed across the Rec. 'What was that?' Steve stopped filming.

'I dunno!' replied Ava. 'A car backfiring perhaps?'

'When did you last hear a car backfire? Modern cars don't do that anymore. Anyway, it came from the woods, not from the road.' Adam looked over to where Robbie had been standing and saw him running towards the footpath, followed by Bradley.

'Gather all the kids up and move them to the other side of the Rec. I'll go and investigate,' shouted Adam as he too started running towards the woods.

He hadn't gone far when he came across Snakey, standing motionless in the middle of the footpath, wide-eyed with shock.

'What happened?' demanded Adam. Snakey didn't reply but just pointed further down the path. 'Join the others on the Rec,' commanded Adam, and once more began to run.

Robbie and Bradley were standing side by side, looking intently at something . Adam halted alongside them and he too saw the shocking sight. It was a man's body, shot through the heart. Jason Prince, the photographer from the Gazette, lay sprawled on the ground and on his chest was a photograph, torn in half and edged with blood, of a very young and half-naked Skye Beattie.

'Please, can you both leave the way you came? Don't touch anything,' instructed Robbie, 'Dad, can you position yourself at the entrance to the wood to stop anybody else coming this way? Keep your eyes open. Whoever killed this man may still be nearby. I'll ring my boss. This is now a murder scene.'

The skies began to darken as if sensing the mood of the day had changed - a portent of doom. It wasn't a lack of curiosity which dissipated the crowd of townsfolk, who stood in groups, whispering and pointing towards the woods; it was the rain, accompanied by a sudden, cold gust of wind, which began to fall and didn't stop for the rest of the evening.

8

Saturday Evening

'Tell me everything,' Ginny said. So Adam proceeded to tell her about the fateful events earlier that day.

'I keep going over the fact that I was standing there in front of a dead body, holding my camera, and yet I didn't take a photograph,' said Adam. 'It didn't even occur to me to take one. It somehow felt invasive.'

'You shouldn't beat yourself up about it,' said

Ginny, 'It would have seemed ghoulish, and it just helps you narrow down the type of photographer you want to be.'

'I took a few photos while I stood guarding the entrance to the footpath, including this one.' Adam passed Ginny his digital camera and showed her an image he had taken using his telephoto lens. It featured Skye Beattie emerging from the woods and looking distraught. 'Do you see? She must have strayed off the path because it looks like brambles have ripped her dress.'

'Where is Skye now?' asked Ginny, 'We never managed to have our meeting. We had arranged it for this morning.'

'I don't think that will be happening. The police took Skye back to the City South station for questioning. There's something else I have to show you. It's all over the internet. Do you remember I told you that I saw three girls leaving the woods just before the shooting? One of them must have posted this. It's gone viral!' Adam searched on his phone and then handed it to Ginny. She watched for a second and then paused the video.

'I presume that person with Skye is Jason, the victim.' Adam nodded.

'That's right. And it's pretty much in the same spot that we discovered his body.' Ginny restarted the video. Skye and Jason were talking. They were too far away for their conversation to be distinct and the sequence was punctuated with stifled laughs from the girls filming it. Ginny watched Jason attempt to pull Skye towards him as if trying to kiss her, and her struggling to get free of him. In doing so, Skye lost her footing and ended up sprawled on the ground at his feet. Jason looked down at her and laughed. Skye struggled to her feet and angrily pushed Jason in the chest. Again, he laughed at her, so she attempted to slap him, but he fended her off easily. Then Skye, obviously realising she was no match for him, turned and disappeared into the woods.

'Looking at when the girls posted it, I would say it was just minutes before Jason's murder,' said Adam.

'For their sakes, it's a good job that the girls didn't see it. But surely the police don't think Skye did it? That dress is so tight-fitting that there's no place to hide a weapon!'

'That's true, but Robbie told me they are trying to ascertain if she aided and abetted the murder. You see, there's another suspect. Her boyfriend, Jay, could have pulled the trigger.'

'Poor girl, it's not exactly the homecoming that she would have expected. Does she have family here?'

'No, according to Ava, she was an only child and brought up by her mother, who died a couple of years ago. Skye and her boyfriend were staying in the Victoria Hotel.'

'And have the police picked Jay up?'

'No, they can't find him. He must have done a runner.'

'Can you get a message to Skye via Robbie from me?' asked Ginny. 'Just tell her to get in touch with me if there is anything I can do to help. For some reason, I just sense that she is innocent.'

***

'As guilty as hell, this one,' sneered Detective Sergeant Bristow.

'She didn't seem like the murdering type to me, Sarge' replied Robbie.

'You're still wet behind the ears, sonny. When you've been in the force as long as I have, you learn to develop a sixth sense.'

I wonder if relying on that sense is the reason you are still a Detective Sergeant and not a Detective Inspector, thought Robbie. However, he knew better than to contradict his boss, so he just nodded.

'She should be waiting for us in Interview Room One. We'll let her stew for a few minutes more. Psychology, see?' Bristow tapped his temple with his forefinger, 'Got to use your brain.' Sometimes, Robbie doubted that Bristow had one and instead just acted from pure animal instinct!

Ten minutes later, once the recording machine was in operation and after the preliminary questions, the interview was in full flow. As was often the case, Bristow had instructed Robbie to keep quiet. Robbie had felt uncomfortable from the start, noticing how his boss had looked at Skye. Her turquoise stretchy bodycon dress, which had looked stunning during the photoshoot, now looked inappropriate in the stark, sterile environment of a police station. It made her look oddly vulnerable, an impression heightened by Bristow's attitude.

'How did your dress get torn? Stand up. Let me see.'

Skye looked towards Price, the duty solicitor, who just shrugged.

Awkwardly and self-consciously, Skye stood, revealing where two gaping rips in her dress exposed her thigh.

'I ripped my dress on some brambles. I lost my

way from the footpath,' she said as she sat down again.

'Are you sure you didn't do it in the fight with Jason Prince? We've all seen it.' Sky looked confused and turned to her solicitor.

'What's he talking about?' There was a whispered exchange during which Bristow sat back and smirked, tapping his fingers on the table.

'I believe you are referring to a film in circulation on social media,' said Price, 'My client refuses to answer any more questions until she has seen it for herself.' Bristow's smile widened, and he reached for his phone. He had the film cued up in readiness for this moment and now he pressed play and pushed the phone towards Skye. He quickly snatched it back when he realised that the film had ended, and it had rolled on to play a movie of a kitten playing with a ball of wool. Bristow scowled at his phone, as if it had made a fool of him on purpose.

'I suggest that had that girl kept filming, we would have seen you return with a gun and shoot Jason Prince in the heart in retaliation for humiliating you.'

'Where would I hide a gun?' Skye held her hands up in exasperation. 'I don't even have a handbag. Ava had all my things.'

'I'm not saying you were in this alone. Tell me.

Where will we find Jay Gordon? We would like a chat with him. When did you last see him?'

'I don't know. I wasn't really aware of him during the day. He doesn't usually come on photoshoots with me because he gets jealous as I need to give all my attention to the photographer. I caught a glimpse of him in the background a few times, but I couldn't put a time to it.'

'So you didn't check if he was around before your - what's the word I'm looking for? Your tryst! Your tryst with Jason Prince.'

'It was nothing of the sort,' snapped Skye angrily.

'Then just why were you skulking in the woods with him?'

Skye hesitated. 'I wanted to ask him about returning some photographs.'

'That doesn't explain why you had to ask him in the woods!'

'Erm, the photos were, erm...private. I wanted to protect my reputation.'

'Hah, well, that's shot to bits now, isn't it,' sneered Bristow. Robbie winced at the Sarge's choice of words.

From then on, the police gleaned very little information helpful to their investigation and they returned Skye to the cells.

'Broome, do you know this Ava that our suspect referred to?'

Robbie nodded.'She works in the post office.'

'Then, by the sound of it, she will have the suspect's phone. Get in touch and get that phone. We can find the boyfriend's number on it and track him down. I thought about asking her for his number, but then I decided not to. Didn't want to risk her alerting him. See, strategy - you can't rush into these things!'

Robbie nodded, thinking, *But how could she alert him if she is locked up in a police cell and doesn't have a phone?*

Then, in an istant, everything changed. The desk sergeant appeared in the doorway.

'Looks like you two had better get yourself over to Shepton Rise as quick as you can. There's been another murder!'

9

Sunday

Ginny couldn't really say that she was enjoying her morning cup of coffee, despite the fact that she was drinking her usual French blend: strength five, with a dash of milk. She was sitting in the conservatory with a view of the garden in which Jackie Carlton, who had recently begun working for her, had done wonders during her once-a-week visits. She had very nearly restored the garden to a level of respectability that even Ginny's parents would have deemed up to their very high standards. Ginny's cat, Tuxie, was sitting on her lap and, judging by the loudness of her purring as Ginny stroked, had no idea that Ginny felt on edge. *It's daft. I hardly knew Skye. I probably met her for a total of twenty minutes. When our lives intersected, I was pleased to offer her a hand to help her rise in her chosen profession, which was ironic because my life was about to spiral downwards. However, with Adam's help and affection, I am climbing out of that. Now Skye will be the one at a really low ebb. I just feel I need to reach out and help, but do I have anything to offer, and would she want me to get involved anyway?*

Ginny's contemplation was shattered by the sound of the doorbell, accompanied by someone knocking loudly. Tuxie leapt off Ginny's lap and darted for the catflap, aiming to continue her nap in a secluded part of the garden.

The knocking continued, so by the time Ginny reached the door, she was feeling somewhat disgruntled. *Okay, okay, I hear you!* When she opened the door, instead of a delivery man with the order of headed notepaper that she was expecting, three police officers were waiting on the step. Only PC Laura Treadmore was in uniform. Laura had helped Ginny in the past and was a good friend of Robbie's. Ginny knew the oldest of the three - it was Robbie's abrasive superior, Detective Sergeant Bristow. The third was unfamiliar but he was presumably in the police force, too.

'Mrs Fellows,' said Bristow.

'DS Bristow,' returned Ginny.

'I am here with DC Cosgrave and PC Treadwell, and we would like to ask you a few questions.' Laura winced. The Sarge never got her name right, but she would be in trouble if she corrected him. Ginny knew that refusing to answer Bristow's questions was not an option. He would take any opportunity to whisk her back to the police station, precisely because he knew how uncomfortable that would make her feel.

'Do come in,' Ginny said politely, leading the party to the conservatory, 'How can I help?'

'Mrs Fellows, I would like you to describe your activities yesterday. Did you leave the house, and if so, at what time?' began Bristow.

'Surely this can't be about that poor photographer who was murdered yesterday? I've never even met him, and I certainly was nowhere near the woods.'

'I think we will get along much quicker if you allow me to ask the questions, Ma'am, and you haven't answered my first one.' Bristow's oily, sarcastic manner never failed to put Ginny's back up. She gritted her teeth.

'I left the house at around ten in the morning and

was driven by Adam Broome to the house of Marcus White. He is ill, and I've been visiting these last few weeks because he was a friend of my father's.' Laura and Cosgrave exchanged glances, which Ginny couldn't decipher. Laura looked apologetic, but Cosgrave gave a smirk. Ginny ignored him and continued. 'Afterwards, I returned home and spent the afternoon catching up on some paperwork. I was on a conference call for an hour from seven, and Adam Broome called around just as it finished and filled me in on the day's events.'

Bristow asked some questions about Marcus, which began to annoy her.

'Look, if you think Marcus got out of bed and went to the woods to murder someone, then you are mistaken. He couldn't walk across the room!'

'As I said before, Ma'am, please allow me to ask the questions,' replied Bristow.

I hate being called Ma'am, thought Ginny.

'Sir, don't you think we should...?' began Laura.

'When I'm good and ready, Police Constable Treadwell,' snapped Bristow. 'Marcus White. He was a newspaperman, wasn't he? So he would be likely to have known the victim, Jason Prince, wouldn't he?'

'I would imagine so. He's the proprietor of the Gazette, but I have no idea how hands-on he has been lately.' *For goodness sake, does he think that he took out a contract for someone to kill the photographer?*

'And do you know how well he knew the model, Skye Beattie?'

Give me strength! 'How would I know that?' protested Ginny, 'Skye was an intern for only a brief period over five years ago. I only met her once myself. Why don't you ask Marcus directly?'

'I'm sorry, but that won't be possible. Unfortunately, I have some bad news for you, Mrs Fellows. Last night, between the hours of seven and eight, someone murdered Marcus White.'

10

Sunday

Ginny stood at the end of her dining room table. Adam and the Dead Actors were seated around it.

'I'm so pleased you could all drop everything and come here,' she began.

'I didn't drop everything - I didn't drop my trousers,' quipped Steve.

'Well, thank heavens for that!' replied Angie, 'I've had enough shocks for one week!'

'I'm afraid there's another one coming,' said Ginny. She forced a smile; although she was almost overwhelmed by sadness. She was glad of the irreverent company; they were always guaranteed to lift her mood. Ginny hadn't told them the reason she wanted them here. She needed them this evening not just for their humour but also because this meeting served to draw a line between the useless despair that had overcome her earlier in the day and the determined resolution she felt now.

'I've already had one shock today,' said Doc, 'United lost five-nil! I had been trying to stay away from the football results all day so I could watch without knowing the score on *Match of the Day* tonight. But I made the fateful mistake of going into town to buy some food for dinner and every person in every shop was talking about it, so I'm glad I don't have to see it now.'

'Serves you right for supporting such a terrible team,' said Steve. 'I was watching a rerun of *The Likely Lads* the other day. The episode when they were trying not to hear the result of an England match.'

'I know the one,' cried Doc, 'Spoiler alert, spoiler alert! They eventually manage it, only to discover the match was postponed.' Julia interrupted Doc and Steve's laughter to stop them from revisiting more scenes from the old TV show.

'One thing I know about Ginny is that she won't have asked us round here to talk about football or a much-loved 1970s sitcom!'

'Sorry, Mrs Fellows,' replied Steve and Doc, using a tone they might have used as naughty schoolboys apologising to their teacher.

'That's alright. I'm happy you are here, but you are quite right, Julia, so I will begin. But first, I have to correct you. You called the show by the name of the 1960s original series, whereas the one you mentioned was called *Whatever Happened to the Likely Lads?*'

'I bow to your superior knowledge,' replied Steve.

'I may not be able to act, but it's my world too,' smiled Ginny. 'Anyway, unlike Detective Sergeant Bristow, I'll come straight to the point. Last night, somebody murdered my friend Marcus White.' The Dead Actors gasped in shock. They hadn't been expecting that! 'He was suffocated with his own pillow.'

'Oh no! Two murders in one day!' gasped Angie.

'And in Shepton Rise!' commented Julia in amazement.

Ginny frowned. 'When that reporter, Jason Prince, was shot, I wondered if I should get involved, if only because I felt sorry for Skye Beattie, but after this morning's news, together with some information that

Adam told me, I can't just sit back. Adam, perhaps you could tell the others what you know.'

'This is a secret. Robbie told it to me, so I told Ginny, and now I'm telling you.'

'It has all the hallmarks of a good secret,' said Angie.

'But it can't go any further,' stressed Adam, 'I think Robbie knew I would share it with you, but no one must know it came from him, or Bristow will have his guts for garters.'

'That's a horrible expression,' mused Julia, 'I wonder if anyone ever did that? I mean, they would be all slippy. They would hardly keep your socks up!'

'I recommend drying them out in an oven set to a low temperature for at least two hours,' suggested Angie. Now it was Julia and Angie's turn to apologise to the teacher:

'Sorry, Sir.'

'There is one detail that the police have not released to the public,' continued Adam, 'I saw the photographer's body. Half of a torn photograph of Skye had been placed on his chest. They asked me not to tell anyone, but on Marcus White's pillow, the murderer had left a copy of the same photograph!'

'So it seems there is a connection between the two

murders,' said Ginny. 'I don't know what it is, but I am determined to find out.'

'I've got a question for you, Ginny.'

'Oh, yes Doc?'

'Who is the murderer?'

Ginny laughed in response. 'If only it were that simple!'

Angie's hand shot up, 'Please, Mrs Fellows. It wasn't me.'

'Well, don't look at me. I get the blame for everything around here,' whined Steve.

'Zen, Madame Julia, j'accuse,' said Doc in an appalling French accent. 'Oh, wait a moment, you were having lunch with me, so it can't have been you.'

'Settle down, gang,' said Ginny. 'A good place to start is to compile a list of who is not the murderer. Look at this video that Adam filmed.' She flipped open her laptop, and the Dead Actors watched the film pan across the Rec, culminating in the sound of a gun being fired.

'I've shared this film with Robbie,' said Adam, 'So now the police can pinpoint the time of the murder. What's more, we can broaden the scope of the investigation because, in order to enter the photography competition, I had to set myself up as the moderator for a group chat room where the kids could post their photos. I've already asked everyone to post all their photos, not just the ones with artistic merit. There will be a lot to trawl through, but I can add you to the group so we can all study them.'

' I appreciate that if we catch the photographer's killer we also get Marcus' murderer, but what do we know about the second one?' asked Julia. 'Was there a robbery, for instance?'

'I'm not sure,' said Adam. 'Robbie doesn't think the murderer ventured into the rest of the house, or the nurse would have heard. The murderer prised open the French windows in Marcus' room.'

'The windows were open when I visited earlier in the day,' said Ginny, 'But the nurse would have locked them later. Marcus had a safe in his room. I don't know what was in it, but he asked me to check if the door was closed. Bradley Steele had brought some papers for Marcus to sign that morning and deposited them in the safe. Marcus said he had fallen asleep before Bradley left, which wasn't unusual, so he didn't see if Bradley had secured the safe. I pulled hard on the handle, and it was indeed locked.'

'Of course, that means your fingerprints are on the safe,' remarked Doc.

'I know. I told Bristow about it.'

'So, the photograph suggests that Marcus knew Skye. Do we know if that's true?' asked Doc.

'There are three ways we can find that out,' said Ginny thoughtfully. 'The simplest thing is to ask Skye herself, but she can be held for at least thirty-six hours without being charged. Even then, the police can apply to a magistrates court for an extension of up to ninety-six hours. That would take us to Monday afternoon. In the meantime, Julia, I wonder if your son, Rupert, could scour the internet and see if he can find a photo of Skye and Marcus together? Marcus attended a lot of charity events - The Rotary Club and the like. Maybe something will turn up.'

'Sure. Rupert enjoys these little investigations for you, Ginny. He uses them as an excuse for asking me to bring his meals to his room so he never has to venture into the real world - unless I drag him kicking and screaming to school!'

'You said three ways, Ginny' prompted Doc.

'Ah, that's where I come in,' said Adam. 'Jason's murder has left the Gazette short of a photographer. Bradley asked me if I would step in until they can advertise for a permanent replacement. I'll see what I can find out.'

'Was Marcus married?' asked Angie, 'You've never mentioned a wife.'

'He was married, but she passed away before I ever met him,' replied Ginny, 'He has a daughter, Margaret, though. They had a massive argument a couple of years ago - I think it was about the Gazette - and they were no longer speaking. However, Marcus did mention that he had recently written to her.'

'Is there anything else we can do?' asked Steve.

'No, I don't think so,' said Ginny, 'It might all be a waste of time, and the police will solve the murder. I'm guessing that the prime suspect is Skye's boyfriend, Jay. However, I can't think for the life of me why he should want to kill Marcus, and that's something I want to explore, but you've all got your work cut out studying all the youth club photos and video.'

'There is something else we can do,' said Doc, delving into a bag at his feet and pulling out a bottle of wine, 'And that is to raise a toast to Ginny, Adam, and the Dead Actors! The Game is Afoot.'

11

Monday

Laura pinned another photograph on the noticeboard at the request of Detective Sergeant Bristow, who was leading the investigation.

'Listen up,' he barked to the assembled police officers, who had been silently waiting for him to speak anyway. 'The Chief wants us to clear this up in double quick time, which suits me fine.

'We have one obvious suspect, this fellow here.' Bristow pointed to a photo of Jay Gordon, 'He's Skye Beattie's boyfriend and he has some previous, just petty offences, and it looks like he's done a runner. Smith! Anything to report?'

'We haven't found him yet, Sir. DC Broome and I visited his room in the Victoria Hotel, and judging by the fact that he hadn't returned to collect his clothes, it looks like he left in a hurry. I've never seen so many expensive designer trainers brought for just a few days' stay, and he's left them all behind. Of course, all Skye Beattie's stuff is there too. The hotel manager is doing his nut because they should have checked out by now, and someone else has booked the room.'

'Well, he'll just have to lump it,' said Bristow. 'Is there anything else of interest in the room? Anything to point to the attack being premeditated?'

'No, Sir, we didn't find anything useful.'

'Where are we with the phones, Cosgrave?

'We confiscated Skye Beattie's phone, which the Post Office girl Ava Nesbitt had been looking after during the photo shoot. We followed up on everyone who contacted her during the day in question, but they were just model agencies. Jay Gordon did not ring her that day. He hasn't rung anyone if it comes to that. I reckon he knew we could track his usual phone, so he's probably bought a burner phone and slung his old one. What is interesting is that he received a two-minute call thirty-five minutes after the photographer was murdered. We don't know who it was, although we know it wasn't Skye Beattie because we had detained her by then.'

'Does he have a vehicle?' asked Bristow.

'Nope. He lost his licence last year through being under the influence. Sky Beattie's sports car is still in the hotel car park.'

'Something else the hotel manager is doin' his nut about?' laughed Smith.

Bristow cut him off: 'Have you tried Beattie's London flat?'

'He's not been back, Sarge. We are in communication with the Met, and they are looking for him. They spoke with the caretaker of the apartments, and we sent Laura down to view the CCTV footage of the communal areas. No one has been back to the apartment since Beattie and Gordon left.'

'How much longer can we detain Beattie?' asked Cosgrave.

'We will have to decide if we are going to charge her by tomorrow afternoon,' said Bristow.

'I bet this is the longest she's ever worn the same clothes for,' smirked Cosgrave. Laura raised a hand.

'Oh, Sir. I perhaps ought to tell you that Mrs

Fellows sent in a tracksuit top and bottoms for her. I inspected them. There was nothing untoward, and I didn't think it would do any harm.'

'Well, you thought wrong, didn't you!' barked Bristow. 'This is our patch. Suspects should be kept feeling vulnerable. Well, I must say, you are going to have to do better than this, Treadwell! Everyone, find Jay Gordon, and let's get this wrapped up!'

A few hours later, DS Bristow knocked on the door of Detective Inspector Williams' office.

'Come in, Sergeant. Have you some good news to tell me?'

'We're at a bit of a standstill, Chief, which is why I wanted to show you this.' Bristow passed a letter to his superior. 'It's from Virginia Fellows.' Bristow couldn't bring himself to call her Ginny.

'Where have I heard that name before?'

'She's that interfering busybody from Shepton Rise who likes to poke her nose into police business, Sir' replied Bristow.

'Hmm. I see Mrs Fellows is asking us to release Sky Beattie and suggesting she lives with her while we conduct our investigations. Do you think that's a good thing?'

'I do, Sir. We haven't got enough on Beattie to

charge her. The testimony from the nurse corroborates that Marcus White was definitely alive when we had her in custody, so she can't be his murderer. We need to focus on catching Jay Gordon before he kills anyone else.'

'You don't need to tell me that. The last thing we need is the press to speculate that there's a serial killer on the loose.'

'So, what I thought, Sir,' continued Bristow, 'Is, seeing that we would have to release Beattie anyway tomorrow, why don't we put her under surveillance? There's a good chance she might lead us to Gordon.'

'Right, let's set the wheels in motion. Do you have a surveillance team?'

'Yes, Sir. I've got two good men. Cosgrave and Cassidy. They can melt into a crowd or blend into the shadows. She will never know they are there.'

12

Tuesday Morning

All the Dead Actors were involved. Doc went to the Victoria Hotel and, much to the relief of the manager, made arrangements for Skye to check out.

'I tell you,' complained Dennis, the manager, 'It's caused me no end of problems, this. I even had to move one couple to a local Airbnb out of goodwill, which wiped out any profits but at least stopped them from leaving me a bad review. The police wouldn't let me enter the room, but I peeked through the door, and they made a right old mess when they were searching.

Clothes strewn everywhere!'

'In that case, I wonder if you have a female member of staff who could assist me? It might be a little distressing for Skye to discover the room like that. Between us, we could pack up Skye and Jay's things.'

'Only too happy to,' replied Dennis, 'The sooner we get the room back in service, the better.'

Meanwhile, Steve, Julia and Angie drove to the City South police station to collect Skye. It was a surprisingly quick procedure, and Skye soon emerged carrying her ruined dress in a carrier bag and wearing a tracksuit that had once belonged to Angie.

'Oh dear,' said Angie, 'I stopped wearing that because it had got too tight, but it looks like two of you would fit inside it! I don't think I've been your size since I was ten! I feel another diet coming on!'

Skye laughed. 'I can't tell you how grateful I was to receive it. Apart from the warmth and comfort, it was reassuring to know that there was someone on the outside who was thinking about me.'

A few minutes later, they all piled into Steve's car and set off for Shepton Rise.

'Ohh! I hate this one-way system,' complained Steve, 'I've missed my turn. I'll have to come off here and double back,' Well practised in high-speed car chases from his time on the *City Beat Blue* TV series, Steve crossed three lanes of traffic and took the exit. 'Let's hope the cops weren't watching!' he laughed, then glancing in his mirror, he furrowed his brow, 'Hmm!' Steve drove the rest of the way to Shepton Rise at a more moderate pace.

'Doc and I were talking about your car, Skye,' he said, 'You would only be able to park for two hours outside Ginny's house without a permit, so what we suggest is that Doc takes it to his house where it can live on the drive.'

'That would be great,' said Skye.

'Are we taking the scenic route?' enquired Julia, puzzled by the convoluted course that Steve was following through the outskirts of Shepton Rise.

'Don't look now, but we've got company. There's been a black BMW following me since I took that wrong turn just after leaving the Police Station. My guess is it's the Old Bill.'

'I suppose it's not surprising that the police want to follow me, but what can we do about it?' Skye asked.

'Just ignore them,' said Angie.

'Or we could have a bit of fun!' suggested Steve.

By the time the four arrived at the Victoria Hotel, Doc and the maid had already packed up all Skye and

Jay's belongings.

'Hang on a minute,' said Skye, and proceeded to rummage in her case. She retrieved an outfit and nipped into the bathroom to change, emerging wearing a pair of jeans and a hoody. She handed the tracksuit to Angie, who went into the bathroom herself. Shortly afterwards, whilst Skye settled the bill, Doc carried all her cases out to Steve's car. The BMW, with one occupant, was waiting at the side of the building, opposite the entrance to the hotel car park, while DC Cosgrave waited opposite the front door of the hotel. Angie now emerged from the side entrance to join Doc who was waiting for her. She had squeezed herself into her tracksuit and had a baseball cap pulled over her eyes. Doc and Angie sauntered across to Skye's sports car in full view of the BMW. They pulled out onto the High Street and then sped as fast as the speed limit would allow in the direction of Doc's house. The policeman on the street was taken by surprise, and the BMW took off in pursuit without him. Cosgrave swore liberally. He clenched his fists in annoyance and was further irritated when a tourist, who looked vaguely familiar, approached him to ask for directions.

'Excusez-moi, s'il vous plaît, pourriez-vous ...erm...could you, me dire le chemin, non, erm...tell me the way de la cathédrale?'

'Cathedral! There ain't no cathedral here.'

'Mais il est dit dans mon guide que la cathédrale de Shrewsbury est...'

'Shrewsbury! You ain't in bleedin' Shrewsbury! This is Shepton Rise!' Steve stood aside to allow the policeman full sight of Julia and Skye laughing and chatting as they left the hotel through the front entrance.

'I gotta go,' said Cosgrave brusquely and pushed past the annoying French tourist, but then, somehow, their feet became entangled, sending Cosgrave crashing to the pavement.

'Mon Dieu!' exclaimed Steve, giving a Gallic shrug and holding out a hand to help the enraged policeman to his feet. 'Well, you might have said thank you, or even merci beaucoup,' muttered Steve, as he watched the policeman scurrying along the street, unsuccessfully trying both to look inconspicuous and catch up with Skye and her companion.

'Who's Cassidy bleedin' chasing then?' grumbled Cosgrave, 'This one's definitely our mark.' He spotted the two women entering a shop. He quickened his pace and studied the shop sign from the opposite side of the road. It had a pink and white gingham background, and in a Western-style script was announced 'Bustin' out all Over.' He was none the wiser. After several minutes, he decided he ought to investigate. He was sure his expenses allowance would be sufficient to make a purchase while surreptitiously observing his quarry.

As Cosgrave stepped through the doorway, a jangling bell dashed any hope of a quiet entrance. His heart fell as he realised he had entered a lingerie boutique.

The shop assistant beamed in delight.

'Welcome to my shop. My name is June. Are you looking for something for the lady in your life?'

'Erm...erm, yes. For my girlfriend. I'd like to buy a bra,' Cosgrave stammered. He could have sworn that he heard giggling coming from behind the curtain to the changing room cubicle.

'What size is she, dear?' asked June.

'She's, erm,' Cosgrave held up his hand in a cup shape, then dropped it, realising it was a wholly inappropriate gesture, 'She's, erm, normal. No, I mean average,' then, using take-out coffee as inspiration, he added. 'She's regular.'

'Are you sure I couldn't interest you in some knickers, love? There's less room for error.' As June was saying this, Skye and Julia emerged from the cubicle. Skye placed a bra on the counter.

'Just my size. I'll have to come back for it; I've left my bank card at home,' and then Skye and Julia were gone.

'I'll have a think about it. I must go,' blurted Cosgrave and, red-faced with embarrassment, he rushed out of the shop only to bump into the French tourist again. Or rather, he thought it was the same man, only this time he seemed to be Spanish.

'Señor, ¿es esta una buena tienda para comprar...?'

'Not now,' yelled Cosgrave, attempting to brush past the man, but instead finding himself once again lying on the pavement. As he picked himself up, he heard the door to Bustin' Out All Over close. The tourist had disappeared but, disastrously, his quarry was nowhere to be seen either. His phone rang. It was Cassidy.

'I've been sitting outside this house for ages. Skye Beattie's car is on the drive, and they have both gone inside. Do you want to make your way over here?'

'That's not them, you idiot,' replied Cosgrave, 'I eyeballed the target from a few feet away, but she gave me the slip.'

'Do you think she was on to you?'

'Nah! I'm a professional, mate!'

13

Tuesday afternoon

'Let me show you to your room, Skye,' said Ginny, 'My friend Adam, who, of course, you met on the photoshoot, helped me get it ready. It used to be my room when I was a teenager. I'm afraid it hasn't been decorated since then. It's clean but a little dated. I bet you are used to swanky designer boutique hotels and all the latest interior design trends.'

'Oh. Don't worry,' replied Skye, 'After being in that police cell, there's nothing I'd like more than being somewhere homely like this. Your house is beautiful.'

'I can thoroughly sympathise with you; I've spent some time in the City South police cells myself.'

'Really?' said Skye incredulously.

'Yes, but that's a story for another day. I was innocent, of course, as I feel in my bones that you are. Now, can I get you anything?'

'I'm so grateful to you for arranging this, but would it seem terribly rude if I went to bed? I found it very hard to sleep in the police station.'

'Not at all, I know from bitter experience what you mean. If you need to freshen up, the bathroom is just along the landing; the Georgians didn't go in for en suites, I'm afraid. I'll be doing some work in my study; look for the kitchen, and go out through the back door into the adjoining building. Sleep well, my dear. I'm afraid the policemen watching the house will have a pretty dull time today.'

'Yes indeed,' laughed Skye, then adding to Ginny's puzzlement, 'Maybe one of them could spend his time researching how bras are sized!'

***

Whilst Ginny was working and Skye was sleeping, Adam spent the time getting the room in the Corny ready for the Tuesday youth club session. He had by now received most of the photographs taken on

Saturday and wanted to ensure that he gave the equipment a thorough test drive. He connected his laptop to the digital projector positioned at the back of the room. No one had used the projector since the 'Pop Corny' cinema club had folded, and the last thing he needed in front of a full room were error messages like *Installing updates…come back next Thursday*, or *Error 007: Permission denied. Fix yourself a Martini, Mr. Bond.* Amazingly, it all worked fine, and Adam had time to tick off the entrants against a list that Ava had given him, before the budding photographers arrived.

'Kelsey,' Adam called, 'I haven't got your photos yet; send me them, and I will add them to the presentation. Deano: yours too.' The last to arrive was Snakey. 'Late, but worth the wait! Can you send me your photos, please?' Snakey pulled a face.

'Go on, Snakey. I'm sure they will be fine,' urged Ava. Reluctantly, Snakey pulled out his phone and transferred the images, and Adam added them to the rest of the presentation.

Adam announced that after the Youth Club session had ended, everyone must send him all the photos and videos they had taken, not just the ones they had selected for the competition. He told them he wanted to create a film presentation to document the event. This was true, but not the whole truth because he, Ginny and the Dead Actors also wanted to inspect them for clues.

Adam enjoyed the next hour immensely. He and Ava had decided that selecting images for the competition would be done by the audience. It was to be a low-tech affair so as not to risk malfunction. When the photographer's work was shown on the screen, they would come to the front of the room. The audience would have the chance to see the photos three times, with Adam operating the laptop. Then they would either give a thumbs-up, two thumbs-ups, or none at all and the photographer simply had to gauge the public reaction to help them decide which photo to submit. Adam was bowled over by the range of approaches and felt immensely proud.

At last, it was the turn of the one youth who seldom embraced group activities; Ava often wondered why Snakey bothered attending the youth club at all! He stood at the front now, fidgeting and squirming. Adam projected Snakey's first photo, and the audience gasped and then applauded. The clapping continued as Adam flicked through all three photos that Snakey had submitted. Each one was of a perfectly framed muntjac deer in the woods. Every photograph received two thumbs-ups from all of the youth club members.

'Snakey, these are fantastic,' said Adam. 'I'll give you my thoughts, seeing as everyone likes them all and you can only enter one. The first one is beautiful. You must have been very still not to frighten it. The deer looks completely calm and relaxed. But the camera has picked up a speck of white in the background. Do you see it by the tree trunk? It's a little distracting. The second one is great, too; you can see the deer is startled. It's a photo full of tension. The white blemish has gone, and then the third one, with the deer leaping away, is a brilliant action photo. Did you disturb it by making a noise?'

'It wasn't me; it was a gunshot,' replied Snakey.

***

Adam had decided that he would continue volunteering to work with the Youth Club kids. A line from a Blur song from the '90s came to him. *It gives me a sense of enormous well-being.* It was true! It did! Then, after he had eaten his sandwich in the park - *Ah! Park life* - it was time to wander down to the Red Lion and join the Dead Actors for their usual early-doors get-together.

'You are Chalky White, and I claim my five pounds,' declared Adam to a man standing at the bar with a newspaper under his arm.

'He laughed, 'I wonder whatever happened to Chalky White!' He was referring to a man who used to visit seaside resorts with a copy of the Daily Mirror tucked under his arm. If people identified him, they won a fiver. 'That was a lot of money in those days; now it won't even buy me a pint of ale.' The man Adam had addressed was Baz Kelly and could loosely be termed a roving reporter, although he did more roving than reporting.

'Have you got a piece in this week's paper?' asked Adam.

Baz shook his head with a wry grin. 'The editor wasn't keen on my scathing takedown of our local MP - called it too incendiary. So all you'll find is a film review. I hear you're stepping in for poor old Jason. Drink?' he asked as Emma, the barmaid, placed a pint of beer on the counter.

'Ta very much. I'll have the same as you,' replied Adam. Baz peered up at the shelf behind the bar and pointed at a large jar.

'I'm hungry. I'll have one of them.'

'What!' exclaimed Emma, 'You're going to eat one of them? No one's ever done that before. I don't even know what they are!'

'Pickled eggs,' said Baz.

'But they look disgusting! They look like a load of eyeballs floating about in who-knows-what.' She gingerly fished one out. Baz held it up level with his face.

'Here's looking at you, kid!'

'So what's your next assignment?' asked Adam.

'I'm going to interview some actor. Ricky Flynn. Maybe you know him.'

'I do. I wouldn't meet him on an empty stomach - and you'll need more than a pickled egg- he likes a drink or two. Speaking of actors, I've come to meet some of my pals in the snug. See you around, Baz.'

Shortly afterwards, Adam passed his phone around the table, pointing out photos he particularly liked.

'And one of the best was this little series,' he said as he reached Snakey's photos of the muntjac. 'Who would have thought that with all the high fashion shenanigans going on, this little creature would be lurking in the woods?'

'Do you mean Snakey or the deer,' laughed Steve.

'What is that speck of white?' asked Doc. 'Can't you Photoshop it out?'

'No, we are not allowed to edit them for the competition,' replied Adam as he enlarged it. 'Hmm, not really sure. It's a bit like in that film I saw last week, *Blow Up,* when David Hemmings thought he saw a body lying on the ground in a photograph he had taken - the more you zoom in, the more distorted it gets.'

'I think,' said Angie, peering at the phone, 'That it looks like a foot. It is. It's someone's white trainer!'

'You're right!' exclaimed Adam. 'Knowing where Snakey took the photo, and that a couple of seconds later the deer was startled by a gunshot, that foot can only belong to the murderer!'

14

Wednesday

'Hello, you found me,' smiled Ginny as she filled the kettle. 'Have you caught up with your sleep? You were in bed for hours.'

'I think so,' replied Skye. 'Actually, it was a bit of a struggle. Too much going on in my head so I kept waking up.'

'I'm making breakfast. Would you like a cup of tea and a piece of toast?'

'Oh, that would be great,' replied Skye. 'It seems a lifetime since I had a decent cup of tea.' She gazed through the window. 'You have a lovely garden.'

'Yes, but I have help once a week from Jackie, my gardener. It's that funny time of year when you don't know how long to let things keep growing, remembering how beautiful they were earlier in the summer, or if they should be chopped down. Jackie's good like that - no sentimentality. Take that lavender at the front, for instance. It was beautiful a month ago and I quite liked the flowers as they were drying and turning brown, but no! Jackie wouldn't have it and pruned them right back. She said they would be all the better next year. There's no point having dead wood in your life... I'm sorry, have I upset you by wittering on about my garden.' Ginny had noticed a tear rolling down Skye's cheek.

'No, sorry. It's not your fault. It's just that something you said touched a nerve.'

'Why don't you tell me about it? I'm a good listener,' said Ginny.

'It's Jay. I'd been having doubts about whether he was good for me, and I had been thinking that maybe I should end things, but I hadn't had the courage to do anything about it, and now I think he's done something stupid, and everything is messed up.'

'What was making you think it was time to

change?' asked Ginny.

'I'm still growing, sorry for the plant analogy, and he hasn't been keeping pace with me. To start with, it was fine, he was a lot of fun. He took me to all the best nightclubs, gave me the confidence to book seats at the finest restaurants and to be quite honest, he's a handsome boy and looked good on my arm.'

'I presume you were paying for the posh nightclubs and fancy restaurants.'

'Of course, but it's not that. I have been earning good money lately. I have aspirations, or I had them. I think they've all gone down the drain now. You see, just because I'm a model and my career is centred on my looks, people jump to conclusions, and it's not fair. Take for instance a girl I went to school with, Aileen. She had really long legs and was a brilliant high jumper. She went on to compete internationally. And then there was a boy who was really small, and I know he joined the rowing team and went on to become a cox on a winning team at the Henley Regatta. In both cases, it was the body they were born with, plus their determination, that helped them excel. Yet nobody accused them of being airheads the way people cast aspersions at me.'

'And you feel Jay doesn't have that same

determination?'

'No, I've tried buying him self-help books, even fiction that might take him from the here and now to somewhere in his imagination. But he never gets past the first page. He thinks he's God's gift to women and has no need to change.'

Ginny nodded. 'I think it was Mark Twain who said, "Those who do not read are no better off than those who cannot read." You said earlier that you think Jay has messed everything up. Is that something you've told the police?'

Skye hesitated a few moments before replying. 'No, I did tell them the truth, just not the whole truth. I don't want to say too much because I don't want to get you into trouble. You have been so kind in letting me stay here.'

'Don't worry about protecting me,' assured Ginny, 'I have my own reasons for wanting to get involved. Can I ask you a question? Did Jay know who Marcus White was?'

'That's funny. The police asked me that, too. He wouldn't have heard his name from me. I haven't thought about him for years.'

'In that case, as long as you promise to tell all of the truth, I would like to invite you to a meeting tonight. They are all people you have met: the Dead Actors - Steve, Doc, Angie and Julia, plus my friend Adam. Please help us get closer to the truth.'

***

'Boring, Boring, Boring, Boring, Boring, Boring!' complained Cosgrave. 'I'm bored!'

'You and me both,' replied Cassidy. 'Still, if Jay Gordon turns up, we'll see some action.'

'Do you reckon we're in a good spot here? We are quite far back.'

'Relax; it's fine. I checked on the map. The garden is completely enclosed by high walls that back onto other properties, so the only way out is from the front. We've got a good view of the garden gate - we can see who comes and goes, but they can't see us. Sweet!' Just then, they were surprised by someone knocking on the roof of the car.

'If it's that traffic warden again, I'll...' Cassidy rolled his window down and was confronted by a man holding two polystyrene containers.

'Ginny thought you might like warming up, so I picked up some soup from the Corner Cafe on my way through town,' said Steve in a very posh English accent, passing two lidded cups through the window. 'Good day to you.' Steve continued on his way to Ginny's house.

Cosgrave's brow furrowed in confusion. He couldn't place the man's voice, but the face looked familiar!

***

'Welcome, everyone,' said Ginny, 'And a very special welcome to our guest of honour, Skye Beattie.' There was a gentle ripple of applause. 'She and I haven't chatted much about the current situation as I didn't want Skye to have to repeat herself. In case you are wary about broaching the subject, I do want to say one thing: Skye has accepted that her boyfriend, Jay Gordon, may be involved.'

'Have you heard from him since you were released?' asked Julia.

Skye shook her head. 'I've had no contact since Saturday morning - the day of the photoshoot. I texted my friends in London, but no one has heard from him.'

'Obviously, the police must be tailing you to see if he turned up here,' commented Angie.

'Honestly, you would hardly know they were there,' laughed Steve.

'I think I ought to say something next,' said Adam. 'When we were in the pub last night, I was showing the others a picture of a deer that one of the youth club boys took near the murder scene a few seconds before he heard a gunshot. We weren't sure if it was a shoe that we could see in the background.' Adam was prepared for this moment. He had taped a piece of white paper to one of the framed photographs that lined the room and connected a digital projector to his laptop.

'Nice kit, where did you get it?' commented Doc.

'It was a bargain. I called in at Bish Bash Fast Cash, you know, the pawnshop in...'

'Guys! Can we get on?' interrupted Julia. She rolled her eyes. 'Boys and their toys!'

'Sorry, yes, I got distracted. Here's the photo... Now, here's a blow-up I made.'

Angie peered at the image. 'Yes, it's definitely a foot or rather a trainer. What's that logo? It looks like an M.'

'I'm certain it's one of these,' said Adam, and projected the image of a white trainer emblazoned with a gold letter M. They are called Momentum.'

'They are definitely out of my price range,' said Steve.

'You only ever wear police-style boots, anyway,' observed Angie.

Adam glanced at Skye. Her eyes were wide with

shock.

'Erm, I had better show you this photograph from the Youth Club collection,' he continued, 'See, in the back of the group is Jay, and do you see what he is wearing on his feet?'

'Momentums,' whispered Skye, 'They are his favourite. He brought three pairs with him to Shepton Rise.'

'Had he collected any of his clothes from the hotel?' asked Ginny.

'No. Nothing. Everything was still there.' There was a pause whilst the implications of Adam's discoveries set in. Then Ginny broke the silence.

'I think we were all prepared for this eventuality. We will have to pass the evidence on to the police. We can't prove Jay did it, but we can prove he was in the vicinity seconds before the shot was fired. So, for me, the question is not who did it but why he did it, and why did he go on to kill Marcus White?'

Skye was trembling now, and close to tears, 'I think it was my fault.'

'Skye, how well did you know Marcus White?' asked Julia.

'I only met him a few times. I went to a fundraising dinner with some people from the newspaper. I seem to remember sitting next to him,'

Julia nodded. 'You did. My son, Rupert, found a photo on the internet. Sorry, I wasn't trying to catch you out; that was why I asked how well you knew him, not if you knew him.'

'The answer is not very well. Ginny told me he was killed at home, but I don't even know where that is.'

'If you don't know why he killed Marcus, have you an idea why Jay wanted to kill the photographer?' asked Julia. 'We've all seen that little video of you tussling with Jason, and I must say, he doesn't come out of it in glowing colours, but is that enough to make Jay shoot him?'

'There is more. I didn't want to tell the police because I thought it would make things worse for me, but I want to tell you.' Just then, Ginny's phone rang.

'Sorry, I should have put it on silent. Oh, it's Robbie. I had better take this.' Everyone could see from the expression on Ginny's face that she had received some surprising news. She said very little, then put the phone down. 'Skye. Skye, please know that you are amongst friends. I don't know many details, but Robbie thought it best for you to hear this news from me. It's Jay. I'm afraid the Police have found him. He's dead. He's been murdered!'

15

Wednesday

Detective Inspector Williams perched on a desk at the back of the operations room and signalled Bristow to start the proceedings.

'Alright, alright. Let's cut the chat. Listen up!' cried Bristow. 'I am pleased to say that Operation Snap Happy is coming to an end. There are some forensic details to wait for to wrap it all up, but for most of us, we can get on with the other cases that are piling up. Heaven knows there's enough of 'em!'

Detective Inspector Williams nodded in

confirmation. The pile of folders on his desk was a visual reminder of how many cases from the summer crime wave that had plagued the city were still to be solved.

'Jones, you were first on the scene. Give us your report,' ordered Bristow. Young PC Jones stood and opened his notebook.

'Sir, at six-thirty this morning, the station received a phone call from a dog walker who had discovered something suspicious in the woods near Shepton Rise.'

'Are these the same woods where the first murder took place?' asked DI Williams.

'No, Sir. They would have all been part of the same forest centuries ago but now they are a mile further north. The locals call them Bluebell Woods. It's a more secluded spot, with a lay-by to park in and lots of paths through it, so people usually drive there to walk dogs. The man who had rung us was still at the scene, a Mr Reed. He hadn't disturbed anything. His dog had been on a lead because he liked to chase pheasants but had alerted him to the body by barking and straining to get at it. Mr Reed was pretty shaken up but had stayed to prevent anyone else from going near it.'

'Good man,' said DI Williams. As PC Jones sat

down, he wasn't sure if the DI was referring to him or the dog walker.

'Cassidy, continue, please,' ordered Bristow.

'We were close at hand because we were observing Virginia Fellows' house. The Control Centre gave us leave to investigate because the description of the victim matched that of our suspect. Indeed, when we arrived, we discovered the body of Jay Gordon. He had been shot in the back of the head, his hands were tied behind his back, and he had been blindfolded.'

'Well, we can rule out suicide,' said Bristow. 'This has all the hallmarks of a gangland execution. Matey here is from London and probably upset someone down there. We know he had some convictions for petty offences in the past, but who knows what he's been up to lately? Frankly, off the record, I don't really care. We will share all the intel with the Met, but I imagine they've got enough on their plate without traipsing all the way up here.'

'I didn't hear that!' laughed DI Williams, 'And what about Skye Beattie?

'Obviously, we've called off the surveillance. We were only there to find Jay Gordon,' replied Bristow, 'But until all the forensics are finished, we may as well ask Beattie to remain in the area in case we get evidence to link her to the murders that we could make stick in court.'

'Did you find the weapon, Sergeant?' asked the DI.

'No Sir, but what we did find in his pocket were these.' Bristow held up an evidence bag, 'More photos of Skye Beattie. One of them has been torn in half and fits the half placed by the murderer on Marcus White's body. So that's it. Case closed. Let's move on.'

***

'As far as I'm concerned, this case definitely is not closed,' declared Ginny. It had been almost lunchtime when the news about Jay's death came through, and they had decided to pause to allow Skye to compose herself. Once the news had sunk in, she had dissolved into tears.

'It's my fault, it's my fault,' she sobbed.

The Dead Actors went in search of food to bring back and eat in Ginny's garden. Julia bought soup from the Corner Cafe, and Doc and Steve both treated themselves to a pork pie from Prime Cuts Butchers. Angie, meanwhile, had been shocked by the snug fit of the tracksuit she had lent Skye. She had decided she needed to go on a diet, so she nipped down to QuickMart and bought a ready-made salad. However, she rather set back her progress by accepting a flapjack that Adam had bought from Heavenly Delights.

Now, everyone was back in the dining room. Ginny reached out and squeezed Skye's hand. Skye returned a half smile as if to say, 'Go on'.

'The evidence looks pretty clear about who murdered Jason and Marcus, but I want to know why he did it. The tussle between Skye and Jason may have been a factor, but it doesn't seem enough. Forgive me, Skye, but I am going to have to be blunt. Was it a romantic tryst with Jason?'

'No, definitely not!'

'Have you ever had a romantic relationship with him?' pressed Ginny.

'No, I thought I had a professional relationship with him.'

'But why were you in the woods, and why did you say earlier that it was your fault?'

'I think I had better start at the beginning,' said Skye softly. 'As you probably all know, I started at the Gazette as an intern, and after sitting in on an interview with Ginny, she kindly introduced me to a model agency, and my career took off from there. I was young and very naive in those days, but I received fantastic guidance and support from the agency, so, as a teenager living in the big city, I navigated my way successfully through some tricky situations. But I hadn't always been like that. When I met Jason at the newspaper, I was easily convinced that he was a top-flight photographer. I've worked with many since then, and I know that wasn't the case, but back then I was gullible. Jason told me that I needed a portfolio of photographs; he wasn't wrong there, and he offered his services for free. He took several photographs, some of which he shot in the newspaper offices. At the time, I thought they were good. However, after a meal and a few drinks, he persuaded me to let him take some glamour photographs in a session that got increasingly risque. To start with, I was partly clothed, but by the end, I was completely naked and in poses that I wouldn't do now fully dressed. The combination of alcohol and his false promises about what the shots would do for my career took away my inhibitions.'

'I can see why you wouldn't want the police to know about this as it would give you a motive,' commented Ginny.

'Oh, there's more,' continued Skye, 'The next day, I told him that I wasn't happy about the photos, but he reassured me that he hadn't printed any out and that he would delete the files. I watched him transfer the photos from his camera to his computer and put them in the bin. 'There! Gone forever', he said. I've since learned that he could have restored them later or left a duplicate set of photos on his camera. Either way, he lied because three months ago, I started receiving blackmail notes, and they included photographs taken at that session.'

'And do the police know about this?' asked Ginny.

'No, but I did tell Jay, and he was very angry. I can remember his words now. He said, 'Somebody is going to get what's coming to them!''

'It looks like he carried out his promise,' said Doc grimly.

'So if you say the police didn't know about the blackmail letters and the photographs, where are they now?' asked Ginny.

'I hid them in the back of a picture frame in my apartment. All except for the last photo. Jay took that.'

'I know why the police want to close the case,' said Adam. 'Robbie said they were struggling to investigate a crime wave from a few months back and the evidence is pretty conclusive; your photographs link the two murders, but I still can't see why Jay would kill Marcus.'

'I honestly have no idea,' replied Skye.

'Nor me,' said Ginny, 'But I have every intention

of finding out!'

16

Thursday

The first things they needed were the blackmail letters and the photos. Ginny gave Doc the task of retrieving them.

'We don't know if the Metropolitan Police are still watching Skye's flat,' Ginny had said, 'Just because our own bobbies have lost interest in the case, we can't be certain that the Met have dismantled their operation. For all we know, they may be applying for a search warrant to look for evidence of Jay's gangland activity. So we can't take any chances. Who's going to go? Skye can't, she has to stay local.'

And so Doc found himself on a train to London the following morning. Ideally, he would have driven a builder's van, but he was worried about the available parking, the congestion charge, and the emissions charge, and he didn't have a van anyway, so the train it was. Doc knew that whilst he looked out of place on the journey with his toolbox and telescopic step ladder, once on the street there was nothing more inconspicuous than a man wearing a high-viz jacket. *You could get away with murder,* he thought. *Maybe that was Jay's big mistake; instead of wearing fancy designer trainers, he should have donned a fluorescent yellow jacket and walked away protected by a cloak of invisibility.*

Doc arrived at Skye's apartment complex and buzzed the concierge.

'Yes?' said the man who appeared at the door, loading a mountain of mistrust onto just one word. Doc had decided he would be a cheerful Cockney, complete with an arsenal of rhyming slang.

'Awright? Maintenance. I hope the lifts are working because I don't want to ball of chalk up the apples and pears.'

'What?' replied the security man, who, although he had lived all his adult life in London, originated from

Nigeria.

'Ain't walking up the stairs,' explained Doc. 'Well, I must get on. Got a lot of work to do around the Smoke this morning, chasing me dog and bone. Gotta change some Thomas Edisons'

'What?'

'Got a busy day 'ere in London, mate. I come to change some light bulbs.'

'Wait.'

'Cor blimey! You gonna let me in, or what?'

'Which apartment?'

Hmm, getting chatty, two words! thought Doc. He pulled a piece of paper from his pocket and pretended to consult it. It was actually a note reminding him to buy toilet rolls, but Doc had memorised the address.

'It's flat 235, mate.'

'Ah! That is the one we are watching for the police on CCTV.'

'I ain't bovvered, mate. I don't mind being on the old custard.' The concierge looked mystified. 'Custard and Jelly, mate - telly! I got nuffing to hide. C'mon, I ain't got all bleedin' day.'

'Elevator over there.'

Once inside the apartment, Doc worked quickly. Skye had described the layout of her apartment, and

Doc immediately took a framed photograph down from the wall - it featured Skye as a little girl, walking in the park with her parents. It was in an old frame with fixings that allowed the back to be removed easily, and Doc retrieved the envelope he had come to London for. He was just about to leave when he heard the door opening. The concierge, flanked by two burly police officers, was framed in the doorway.

'What are you up to?' one asked. Doc decided to drop the cheeky chappy persona. They didn't look like they had a sense of humour!

'Had to fix the lights, mate. See.' Doc held his breath and flicked the light switch, praying they would come on. They did, and rows of downlighters illuminated the apartment.

'Let me see in your toolbox.' Once more, Doc held his breath as he flipped open the lid. Before he had left home, he had cut a piece of card to fit the bottom of the toolbox, and Skye's envelope was hidden beneath it. On top were a few tools and an array of different lightbulbs. Doc hoped the policemen wouldn't notice that none of them matched the ones in Skye's apartment.

'I was just on me way,' said Doc.

'Go on then,' grunted the policeman.

'So now you can't give me a ticket for havin' a faulty rear light coz they is all workin',' chirped Doc as he skipped out of the door.

17

Thursday

'There's something I've got in mind, but it might be dangerous, so none of you should feel pressured to do it,' said Ginny.

'Oh, yes?' said Steve, intrigued. 'I don't mind a bit of danger. It's good for the circulation.'

'I had a brief word with Joey before this meeting. Joey runs the Fit for Life gym in town.' Ginny explained to Skye, 'He originally came from London and had what can be only described as a history. Anyway, all that's behind him now, but he still knows people in London who operate on the wrong side of the law. In fact, I've got one particular individual in mind, his cousin Cee Cee. We need more background information about Jay. If Cee Cee would be willing to meet you, I wondered if one of you would be prepared to travel down to London and quiz him about Jay. Joey said Cee Cee generally knows about everything and everyone on the shady side of the street.'

'I'm your man,' said Steve.

'No, you're not!' cried Angie.

'Why not?' replied Steve.

'I'll tell you why not,' said Angie, 'What do most strangers think when you walk into a room?'

'I suppose they think I'm a policeman.'

'Exactly. And who are people like Cee Cee least likely to want to talk to? Policemen! I'll go!' said Angie emphatically.

'But it might be dangerous,' argued Steve.

'So? Do I detect a patronising tone to your reasoning?'

'Erm!' Steve backed down, and so it was settled. Angie was going to undertake the mission, and on the same day that Doc travelled to London, Angie also ventured South, only much later in the day. The inhabitants of London's underworld weren't early risers.

Angie walked through the entrance. It was exactly the kind of place Angie had been expecting. The address was a slightly run-down dry-cleaners. A long counter ran the width of the shop, behind which two young girls were admiring each other's false nails. Signs were pinned to the walls declaring, *All items are cleaned at the customer's risk* and *Garments left uncollected for more than 30 days may be disposed of.* Angie particularly liked the sign: *We cannot be held responsible for lost or damaged buttons.*

'Sorry, we aren't accepting any new orders at the moment; we've got a bit of a backlog,' said one of the girls, indicating the rack of garments in protective polythene bags behind her. Angie noticed the extraordinary number of CCTV cameras in the shop. *Obviously, making sure that no buttons escape unnoticed,* she thought.

'Actually, I have come to meet Cee Cee. He's expecting me. His cousin Joey spoke to him.' The sales assistant raised her eyebrows in surprise and opened the door to a back room. Angie saw a couple of men inside. *Security, no doubt, guarding all the buttons that they have snipped off garments.* One spoke briefly on his phone, then came out of the room and addressed Angie.

'Come.' He opened another door, and Angie saw a staircase beyond. On the next floor, a number of bored looking youths lounged on an assortment of mismatched furniture. The man said, 'Wait', knocked on a door leading from the landing and went in. The youths eyed Angie curiously. Her guide returned and said, 'OK', indicating with a slight nod of his head that she should enter. *It's been nice talking to you,* Angie thought, as he followed her in.

This room was very different. One wall was a deep red; the others were painted black. A Samurai sword was mounted on the red wall. Framed photographs of rappers adorned the room, or at least Angie presumed they were rappers judging by the poses they struck, by the number of tattoos per square inch and by captions like Levi Cipher and Jaxon Blaze. It wasn't really an office; it was more of a lounge. Cee Cee, wearing a black singlet, several heavy gold necklaces, and what looked like the same brand of trainers that Jay Gordon had favoured, was standing in the centre of the room with his hands on his hips and his legs astride.

'You want me to search her, Cee Cee?'

'Ah, come on,' cried Angie, holding her light-weight jacket open. 'Where am I going to hide a weapon?'

'You might be from the cops; you could be wired up.'

'Well, I'm not. Do me a favour!' *Surely technology has moved on, I wouldn't have wires threaded through my jacket?*

'You're alright, leave us now, Jax.' After the door had closed behind Jax, Cee Cee continued to stare at Angie. *Is he trying to intimidate me?* Then he spoke:

'You know, I'm usually good with names and faces. It helps in my line of work: know thine enemy. An ancient Chinese general first said that, you know. But you look familiar, yet I don't think we have ever met. It's putting me on edge. You're not a TV reporter doing a documentary, are you? If you are, I'm not interested.'

'No, but I was in a TV soap for a long time.' Cee Cee's eyes widened in recognition.

'June!' he exclaimed, 'June from *The Street*. Oh, man! I watched it with my mum from when I was a little boy. I can't believe it! June from The Street here in my room. Oh, she would have been so pleased if she knew. I tell you, I was thankful that she didn't get to see that day when you died - when the train crashed into your cafe. She passed away a week before. She knew there was something big going to happen, but she figured you were going to get married. I felt like I lost two people that month, you know.' Cee Cee paused and his eyes started to glisten.

'Do you mind if I give you a hug?' asked Angie, 'My life changed then too.' Cee Cee didn't move, so Angie took the initiative, stepped forward and wrapped her arms around him. At first, he stood rigid but then melted into her. Just then, there was a knock on the door. Jax stepped into the room.

'Hey Cee Cee, oh, sorry.' Cee Cee and Angie broke apart.

'How many times have I told you? You have to wait after you knock?' said Cee Cee.

'Your boss has certainly got a way with the ladies,' said Angie with a wink.

'Sorry, Cee Cee. It can wait.' Jax closed the door behind him.

'Hey, take a seat, June' said Cee Cee, pointing to one of the matching black leather sofas. He sprawled on the other. 'Do you still watch it?'

'Not often,' replied Angie. 'Sometimes it hits a nerve. I keep in touch with some of the cast, though. How about you?'

'Well,' he drew the word out, 'Well, I'm here when it's on. I wouldn't watch it in front of the boys in any case, but I use catch-up. Late at night, on my own. It's like being in communion with my mum, you know what I mean.' Then he laughed. 'Ha! So, if you want to know what's been going on in *The Street* over the last few years, I'm your man. Anyway. What brings you here to see me, June?'

18

Thursday

Whilst Angie and Doc headed down to London, Adam made the short journey across to Cranthorpe to start his first day as a temporary photographer for the Gazette. He knocked on Bradley Steele's office door.

'Come in, my man! Lauren told me you were here. Take a seat.'

'I'd like to say, first of all, thank you for giving me this opportunity to work on the paper, but I'm so sorry for the circumstances that led to the vacancy.'

'Ah, yes. A terrible business, but thankfully, the

man who committed those murders appears to have met his nemesis so we can all sleep easy in our beds.' Adam nodded in agreement.

'I can't promise that the post will be permanent,' continued Bradley, 'Staffing decisions are outside my remit. Our main objective is to put out the best paper we can.'

'I'll try my best. Where do I start?'

Bradley slid a list across the desk.

'Recent events mean we will be running a feature on the murders, so we will need some location photos of where they occurred. Given that Marcus was our proprietor, we will be treating the coverage of his murder with sensitivity out of respect for his family. There will be no gory details in the copy. All we require from you is a long-distance shot of his house.'

'I quite understand.'

Then after that, there are two main features. Firstly the dratted roadworks; see if you can get a photo that shows a multitude of traffic cones and nobody at work. Also, you need to be available to cover the Under-Twelves' football match on Sunday. The coach owns one of the local garages, and he is one of our major advertisers, so try to get a shot of them scoring a goal.'

'I'll get right on it.'

'Go and sort your paperwork out with Lauren - your National Insurance number and the like. She'll find a desk for you, and I do believe the police have returned Jason's camera, so you're welcome to use it. It's good to have you on board, old chap!

After Adam had given Lauren his details, he followed her into the newsroom.

'If you don't mind, I'd rather not sit at Jason's workstation,' he said. 'I know I wouldn't be here now if he were still alive, but sitting at his desk seems a bit creepy. I won't be trying to copy what Jason did; I hope I've got something of my own to offer.' Adam was standing quite close to Dillon's desk, and he could have sworn that he heard Dillon mutter: 'Thank God for that.' Lauren seemed oblivious to the comment and said, with a sweeping gesture:

'Can you see how we've tidied up? It was quite a mess when you came before.

'My desk wasn't,' said Dillon defensively.

'No, yours wasn't,' conceded Lauren. 'It was our way of dealing with what happened. It all started with Bradley at the weekend. He got rid of that tatty old rug in his office. Bald spots everywhere. It used to block up the vacuum cleaner. He said it was handmade and unique. Uniquely tatty, if you asked me. The new one is so much better. '

'I couldn't put my finger on what was different,' exclaimed Adam, 'The old rug was mostly red, wasn't it, and the new one is more blue. The whole place looks spruced up. I can see why you have done it. A new broom, as the saying goes. Like me.' Lauren just looked at him. 'Broom, I'm Adam Broome. Oh well. Well done! I think I'll sit over there by the window. Nothing like a room with a view, even if it is a view of the SpeedyFix Tyres garage!'

'You will be sitting at the desk next to Baz,' said Lauren, 'He won't disturb you much; he takes the term 'roving reporter' to the extreme.'

'Oh, I've met Baz a few times down the Red Lion. He's quite a character!'

'It doesn't surprise me,' laughed Lauren wryly,' I bet someone says that in every pub in town. Anyway, here's your login code: four letters followed by four numbers. Change it to something memorable once you are in the system. All the computers are networked together, so it's easy for you to share your photographs. Dillon will give you a hand if you need it.' Dillon nodded without taking his eyes off his computer screen.

Rather than rushing off to take photographs, Adam decided to conquer the technology first and fired up the computer. *First things first, I might as well change my password.* It was a fairly straightforward operation and to keep things simple he used the four letters of his name and the year he was born; *I'm hardly going to be hacked by some foreign power trying to steal photographs of the roadworks on the bypass!*

'Can you tell me what this folder called *Shares* is, please?' he called to Dillon. Although he didn't make eye contact, Dillon finally looked in his direction.

'It's the network. You need to create and share a password for it. Then, we can all access the files in that folder. I tell you what. This might be useful. He wrote on a scrap of paper and handed it to Adam. 'This was Jason's shared folder. I don't know if it's still on the system. Bradley may have deleted it, but I doubt it.'

Thanks, Adam thought. *This could be useful indeed!* Access to Jason's files proved helpful to Adam in a professional sense. He got hints about how to frame action photos of the Under-Twelves' football matches, but he was determined to take a more interesting photograph of the roadworks than Jason did. *It's just a pity I can't find anything that will interest Ginny and the Dead Actors.*

19

Thursday Evening

'How was your first day at work, Adam?' asked Julia. The Dead Actors were all assembled in Ginny's Operations Room, otherwise known as her dining room, to share what they had discovered.

'It was great, thank you,' replied Adam. 'Although, I don't think I've much to add to our investigation. I was greeted by Bradley, who was very welcoming, and Lauren, who seemed very efficient. Baz breezed in but then went off for lunch and never came back.'

'A liquid lunch at the Red Lion, no doubt,'

commented Doc.'

'I met Dillon again, although he's hard to get chatting to. I'm not sure if he is unfriendly or just shy. One thing I learned, though, is that I don't think there was any love lost between Dillon and Jason. I asked Lauren about it when we were alone. She didn't say anything; she just pulled a face. I tell you, her face was a picture, and they say a picture is worth a thousand words!'

'Ah, dear old Kojak,' said Julia as Steve and Doc began to recite the words to Telly Savalas' hit version of *If*.

'We need lollipops to solve this case!' declared Angie.

'Is that a new camera you've got there, Adam?' asked Doc.

'Yep,' certainly is. It's beyond my price range. It belongs to the Gazette. Jason had it before me; before you ask, it still has photographs stored on it - none, however, of much interest. He took a lot of Skye, as you might imagine. The only useful thing, as far as I can see, is that the time is recorded when a photo is taken. For instance, ten minutes before he was murdered, he snapped Skye from a distance on the Rec.'

'That's right,' said Skye, 'I saw him photograph me, and then he pointed to the footpath leading to the woods.'

'So, that's it, I'm afraid; a good day for me but not much use to you guys!' concluded Adam.

'My turn now,' said Doc as he laid out the contents of his toolbox on the table.

'The light in my porch has blown; I think this would fit it!' said Angie, holding up a light bulb.

'That's not what you are supposed to be looking at,' said Doc wearily.

Ginny studied the photos first, picking one up and looking at it closely.

'I see they are all the same image. They don't look like they have been commercially printed, which is not surprising. Was the photograph that Jay had the same as these?'

Skye nodded. Ginny took a sheet of paper from the pile on the table.

'This certainly conforms to what you would expect a ransom note to look like,' she said, 'Individual letters have been glued onto a piece of printer paper, the kind you would find in a million offices, and they appear to be cut from a newspaper.'

Adam was at her side. 'I am fairly certain they have

been cut out of the Gazette. I've spent quite a lot of time studying the typefaces they use.'

'That narrows it down a bit,' laughed Doc. 'So it's someone from Cranthorpe, Shepton Rise, or one of the surrounding villages.'

'It's a start,' replied Ginny, 'I wonder what's on the back of the newsprint? Maybe we could work out the date it was published. I'm not sure why it might help, but at this stage, we just need to accumulate information, and then we can figure out what it all means.' Ginny attempted to peel off one of the letters. 'That's no good; it's going to rip.'

'I have an idea,' said Doc. 'I wonder if there is a specialist scanner that might show us what's on the back of these letters. I know just the guy to ask.'

'I didn't know you were a techno whizz,' remarked Adam.

Doc grinned and shook his head 'I spent years as an actor working on *Emergency Level Red*,' he explained to Skye. 'The production team took special care to make sure all the equipment looked genuine, even though it was often mocked up. Carl from props used to bring in a guy who worked in sales for a medical equipment company as a consultant. Carl still works on the series, so I'll give him a ring to get the contact details.'

'Julia, you've been studying the Youth Club photographs. Have you anything to report?' asked Ginny.

'I'll be very brief. I've gone through all the photos taken on the Rec before the murder and, aside from a few of the youngsters - I'm sure we can count them out as I doubt they would have the means to acquire a handgun - the one person who did not feature in anyone's photos, apart from Jay and Jason, was Dillon. Also, Rupert found another photo taken at that charity dinner. See, Marcus is sitting next to Skye. Everyone is smiling and laughing with one exception. Just look at that expression of hatred and animosity. It's Dillon!'

'How did you get on, Angie,' asked Ginny. 'I must say, I'm pleased to see you safely back in one piece.'

Angie had already decided not to reveal the first part of her meeting with Cee Cee. That was a tender and private moment between the two of them.

'It was a little uncomfortable at first, and I'm sure I wouldn't have been let through the door if it were not for Joey's introduction, but in the end, Cee Cee was very frank and honest.'

'I thought you said his name was Cee Cee, and now you're calling him Frank,' interjected Steve.

'Ignore him!' urged Julia, 'Go on, tell us about the lion's den, Angie.'

I'll skip the preamble. I hope this isn't going to be painful listening for you, Skye.'

'I think I'm all cried out.'

'Another good song!' cried Steve.

'Steve!' warned Julia in a low voice. 'It's not a good time for a sing-song. Go on Angie.'

'Cee Cee told me that Jay was somebody they laughed about amongst themselves; kind of all style and no substance. It was all an act. But there are two important things I learned. Cee Cee left the room during our meeting, I guess because he didn't want me to overhear a conversation. When he returned, he told me that a source had told him that Jay had recently bought a Russian-made Baikal handgun and several 9mm rounds.'

'That's interesting,' said Ginny. 'Robbie told me that the police recovered a 9mm bullet from Jason's body.'

'Jay said he needed expenses,' said Skye, 'I used to lend him my bank card, even though sometimes he could be a bit extravagant. I didn't realise until I checked my bank account today that he withdrew a thousand pounds.'

'You could buy a gun with that,' said Doc.

Angie nodded. 'The other thing Cee Cee said was that no one he'd asked knew of any reason why a hit squad would be sent to deal with Jay. Cee Cee said that, personally, he would never venture further north than Watford and would simply wait until Jay stepped back on his patch. Speaking hypothetically, of course.'

'Of course,' echoed the other Dead Actors.

'If he hears anything, he will let me know.'

'Well done, Angie,' said Steve, 'You've done far better than I could have.'

Angie tried to visualise Steve giving Cee Cee a hug, then shook her head to dispel such an unlikely image.

'Thank you all,' concluded Ginny. 'It's going to take me a little time to make sense of all this. A glass of wine, a cat on my lap, and time to think is what I need.'

'A pint of beer and a packet of peanuts at the Red Lion is what I need,' said Adam. Anyone care to join me?' The Dead Actors couldn't get out of the door fast enough!

20

Friday

Doc arrived at Ginny's house just minutes before the salesman from Scanülike.

'Goodness! I didn't realise he would come so quickly. He said he was in the area and had a demonstration model in his van,' said Ginny. Then the doorbell rang.

'Ginny, meet Dan. Dan the scan man!'

'Pleased to meet you, Ginny. It's been a long time, Doc.'

'Are you still advising *Emergency Level Red*?'

'Yes, I still pop in now and then. As our equipment gets smaller, the dummy machines on set get bigger, with twice as many knobs and flashing lights.'

'Look, I hope we aren't going to waste your time because we are unlikely to be able to afford one of your scanners, but we would love to see one in action,' said Doc, apologetically.

'No worries, you're a mate, and I was nearby. I've got an appointment at the City Hospital later. You know me, I'll do anything for a nice cup of tea and a biscuit!'

'Hint taken,' said Ginny.

Later, with a mug of tea in hand and the scanner on the dining room table, Dan was all set.

'It would be a dereliction of duty if I didn't give you the spiel,' he said, 'This little beauty utilises a low dead space, high-definition, lightweight, and rugged panel design that is crucial when developing a confidential render-safe procedure.'

'Really?' said Doc, assuming an expression of intelligent interest.

'Absolutely. When every detail is critical, discretion is important and fast reaction is essential - you need a lightweight, tactical solution.'

'I couldn't agree more!' said Doc.

'Moreover, it's easy to carry and conceal, with fast setup and threat detection. It's a discreet, portable DR solution for special operations when you're on the move and need to quickly assess threats.'

'It sounds just the ticket.'

'But when all's said and done, it's just a scanner. Come on, let's give it a go.'

It took three attempts before they obtained a legible copy of what was on the back of the letters glued onto the ransom note.

'That's amazing! Would you mind doing the others?'

'Certainly, I can see myself moving from hospital dramas to advising TV detectives! It's exciting. I'll transfer them to your laptop by wi-fi.'

'And as a reward, as we can't afford to buy your scanner, I'll nip down to Heavenly Delights and get you some more biscuits,' said Doc.

'It's a deal. These are to die for,' mumbled Dan through a mouthful of crumbs.

'Oh, I hope not! We've got enough to deal with as it is!' exclaimed Ginny.

***

Ginny rang Adam. When he answered, she could

hear traffic sounds.

'Oh dear, Adam. I hope this isn't a bad time to call. It doesn't sound like you are in the newsroom.'

It's alright, Ginny. I'm actually lying on my stomach on the pavement, trying to get a dramatic shot of the traffic cones at those roadworks on the bypass. But I think I've got what I need, so I can head back. How was the scanning demo?'

'It was excellent. That's why I'm ringing. We have isolated the text from the back of the letters stuck to the ransom note and are ninety-nine point nine per cent sure that they have been cut out of the Gazette. I wondered if there are digital copies of all the recent editions of the newspaper. It would be a lot easier to search for the snippets of text on a computer than on hard copies in the library.'

'I'll ask when I get back. Perhaps Julia's lad, Rupert, could do the donkey work,' suggested Adam.

'I'm one step ahead of you; I've already asked him, and he said yes!'

***

Lauren beckoned Adam into her office.

'It'll be easier for me to show you on my computer,' she said, 'I only got the hang of it all during the last year.'

'How long have you worked here, Lauren?'

'Oh, longer than I care to think. It was before Bradley Steele came. In fact, before the editor before him started. Life got a whole lot more technical when Bradley arrived. We joined the digital age! Anyway, you need to log on and then go to this folder here.'

'I clicked on that one, but it wouldn't open.'

'Probably my fault. I haven't added you to the user list. I'm sure Bradley won't mind. It could be useful for you to see what's gone before.'

'What's that other folder?' asked Adam.

'That's the data bank for the CCTV. Bradley had it installed after that horrible break-in a few years ago. The files are read-only. You won't be able to change anything. I never look at them myself. They are extremely boring, like watching paint dry. I'm sorry, I don't know how to take them out of your folder.'

'Never mind,' laughed Adam, 'I can ignore them, like you!' *But I won't,* he thought. *When there's no one around, I think I'll take a little look at the recording of Jay visiting the Gazette. In the meantime, I'll email a batch of archive newspapers to Ginny.*

Adam had a quiet period over his lunch hour. Baz was doubtless in the pub, and Dillon was visiting Ava to ask about her recollections of the murder in the woods. Adam opened the CCTV file, selected a date, and settled down to watch the recording with a pencil in one hand and a homemade ham sandwich in the other.

At first, the lobby is empty. The TV screen mounted on the wall, tuned to the BBC rolling news channel, shows candidates for an upcoming byelection. Then Jay enters the Gazette offices and bangs on the reception window. He appears agitated and waves his hands around, and although there is no sound on the recording, you can see that he is shouting. Then he leaves the reception window, moves down the corridor and flings open Bradley's door. The office is presumably empty because Jay carries on to the newsroom and out of shot.

Adam switched to footage from another camera.

Jay strides into the room, walking quickly. His fists are clenched, and his shoulders are tensed. There is only one other person in the room: Dillon. Jay stands before him, thumps on the table and speaks. Dillon points to Jason's empty desk and there is a conversation. Jay appears to relax a little as Dillon writes something on a piece of paper and hands it to him. Jay stuffs the paper into his pocket. Lauren comes into view, hovering nervously in the doorway. Then she evidently hears something, turns her head, and leaves.

Adam flipped back to the first camera and saw that Bradley had arrived.

Lauren points to the newsroom, and Bradley rushes towards it. He confronts Jay. Whilst Bradley is more than twice Jay's age, he is clearly the stronger of the two, and Jay's attitude is less aggressive now. They converse, and then Jay picks up a pencil and writes something down on a piece of paper, which Bradley takes. Then, the editor gently but firmly guides Jay out of the offices.

Well, what to make of all that? Maybe Ginny will make sense of it!

***

Adam and Ginny sat opposite each other at the kitchen table, each with a cup of tea. Adam had called in after finishing work for the day at the newspaper.

'I have a good picture in my mind of the team at the Gazette,' said Ginny, 'I've seen them all in the various photographs and videos taken on the day of Jason's murder, except one. You've often spoken about Lauren, but I don't believe I know what she looks like.'

'There was a glimpse of her in the film I took just before we heard the gunshot because I had just been talking to her, but I'll describe her to you,' replied

Adam. 'Let me see. Her eyes are quite striking because they are violet. They are rather like Elizabeth Taylor's. She has a lovely, radiant smile; it reminds me of Audrey Hepburn's. Her hair is red and tumbles down to her shoulders. It's very much like Rita Hayworth's. Her voice, though, is more reminiscent of Lauren Bacall's: low-pitched, deep and smoky. What else? She has nice hands. I noticed them when she was showing me something on the computer. She reminded me of Grace Kelly at the time. I can't think of anything else, oh no, I can - her legs. She came in quite a short skirt once, and I couldn't help but notice that her legs reminded me of Farrah Fawcett's, you know, in that iconic swimsuit poster. That's about it if it helps.'

'Well, you certainly seem to have taken an interest,' replied Ginny sniffily. Adam remained deadpan for a full five seconds before dissolving into laughter.

'Ah, had you going there, didn't I? Actually, she doesn't look anything like that,' he admitted, flattered that Ginny was feeling jealous.' Ginny smiled ruefully. She really mustn't rise to the bait so easily. She reached across and patted Adam's hand, which was resting on the table. She left it there a moment longer than she needed to, and he twisted his hand round to hold hers and squeezed it. Then, feeling a little overcome, he pulled it away and reached for his phone.

'I'll show you what she looks like,' he said, 'She's about our age. A little bit shorter than you, perhaps. Photos of all the staff are on the Gazette's web page. Here she is, Lauren Spiller.' Ginny stared at Lauren's image. She squinted as she tried to visualise her as a younger woman.

'Does she come from around here?' she asked.

'Lived in Cranthorpe all her life, she said. Working for the Gazette was her first job, and she stayed put.'

'I wonder; she looks familiar. I remember knowing someone called Lauren when I was in the Girl Guides, but I can't recall her second name. Maybe Spiller is her married name anyway. The Lauren I knew went to the Catholic School in Cranthorpe, so you probably wouldn't have met her before. If she is the Lauren I'm thinking of, I haven't seen her since we were fourteen. We've got a lot to catch up on! I'll give her a call at the Gazette.' By way of an answer, Adam broke out into song.

'Ging gang goolie goolie goolie goolie watcha, Ging gang goo, ging gang goo.'

21

Friday

Adam decided he deserved a swift half before going home to cook Robbie's dinner and found the Gazette's roving reporter standing at the bar of the Red Lion.

'Would you like a drink, Baz? How did you get on interviewing Ricky Flynn?'

'I think, from what little I can remember of the evening, that it went well, and I'm pretty sure I've got enough to write a piece. To tell you the truth, the longer the evening went on, the less coherent my notes became. It wasn't any better when I listened to what I had recorded on my phone. Most of the time, I seemed to be roaring my head off with laughter.'

'Ah! Ricky is never more than a few paces away from having a good time!' laughed Adam. 'What did you get up to?'

'Ricky took me to Lloyds cocktail bar. Actually, its real name is Cell U Lloyd, but everyone calls it Lloyds. They specialise in film nights. Do you know a film called *The Thin Man*?'

'Sure I do, with William Powell and Myrna Loy as the detectives: Nick and Nora.'

'That's the one. Well, every time Nick had a drink, all of us watching had to have one too. Perhaps not the best preparation for an interview! Anyway, Ricky was very generous, poured me into a taxi, and paid for it to bring me all the way home from London.'

'That sounds like Ricky,' laughed Adam.

'And how have you found your first week at the Gazette?' asked Baz.

'I'm enjoying it a lot, but the week's not over yet! I've got the Under-Twelves' football match to come!'

'Ah yes, the highlight of the week!'

'To be honest, I'm surprised there hasn't been

more coverage of the murders, but Bradley doesn't want to disrupt the cosy image of life in Shepton Rise,' said Adam.

'It doesn't surprise me. Our local readers don't want to read about Londoners coming up here and killing people; they want to know about the roadworks on the bypass and what can be done about flytipping.'

'But I still don't understand why Jay wanted to kill Marcus Steele.'

'Life's too short, my friend. When I was younger, I used to rush around trying to find out why things happened, but these days, I'm happy enough just to report what happened and leave it at that.'

'Have you always worked at the Gazette?'

'No, I started as an apprentice in Fleet Street, then we moved to Wapping and promptly went on strike. Later, as you'll remember, there was the scandal of Robert Maxwell, who owned the Mirror Group, using company pension funds to prop up his business and by then, to be frank, I was burnt out. So, when the job at the Gazette came up, I happily took a drop in wages in order to protect my sanity. Not that there aren't rivalries and political undercurrents going on there, but I stay out of it.'

'You mean like how Dillon didn't get on with

Jason?' probed Adam.

'Yeah, no love lost there, nor with Marcus, either.'

'Let me buy you another drink. What happened with Dillon and Marcus?'

'I don't know the whole story; all I know is that they had a bit of a barney about work. Then one evening, I was coming back from The Pheasant - they used to have a Tuesday Pie night - and I bumped into young Dillon.'

Didn't Marcus live just around the corner from The Pheasant?'

'That's right, well Dillon wasn't quite right in the head that night. I think he was on medication, and maybe he hadn't been taking his tablets because it was hard to get any sense out of him, he was ranting and raving that much. Anyway, the bag he was carrying knocked against the lamp post, and made such a clang that I asked him what was in it. He said that it was a brick and he would either wrap it around Marcus' head or toss it through his window. Well, I couldn't have that, so I offered to carry his bag and kept him talking until we were safely past Marcus' house. Eventually, after dumping the bag, I ended up walking him home. That last few yards were hard going; he was almost dead on his feet, so I found his keys in his pocket, let us both in and laid him out on the sofa. Funnily enough, there was a big photo of Skye Beattie on the wall. The next day, it was as though nothing had happened.'

'He seems a bit odd, but not that bad now,' commented Adam

'Scratch the surface, and you never know what you are going to find. Well, it's time I was getting off. I need some kip to recover from a night out with Ricky Flynn. See you!'

'I'll have to get going myself. People say an army marches on its stomach, but so does the police force, so I had better get the dinner on before our Robbie gets back.'

Later that evening, Ginny sent Adam a text asking if he could drop by to help with a query she had.

'Rupert has been working hard trying to identify the newspapers from which the ransom notes were cut, and he's come up with the goods on all but one,' said Ginny.

'Really? Good for him. So was the odd one out from a different newspaper?' asked Adam.

'No, that's the curious thing: it still matches the Gazette in style. With the others, the newspaper's date ties in with the day the blackmailer posted it to Skye.

We can tell that by the postmark on the envelopes. So, Rupert knew approximately when the paper would have been published, and he thought he had found it. The content on page two of the newspaper matches exactly the text on the back of the ransom note, but none of the letters on the other side were there.'

'That is strange,' replied Adam, 'I've brought my laptop with me. They have a very sophisticated network for a small provincial paper, and I should be able to access the system from here. It means I can save a photograph or a reporter can file a story without having to return to the office. I'll take a second look.' Adam opened his laptop and began to type in his passwords while Ginny put the kettle on.

'Have you got room for a biscuit?' Ginny said, setting the tray down.

'I could make room,' replied Adam, smiling. 'Aha! Found something. Look! There's a folder I hadn't noticed. It's called FENP. What could that stand for?'

'Flying Elephants Need Parachutes,' suggested Ginny.

'Possibly.'

'Frogs Enjoying Nocturnal Parties?'

'An excellent suggestion, but unlikely. It contains several archive newspapers, including one with the same date as the paper that Rupert found, but the front page is different. Hmm! FENP. I'm sure I can find out tomorrow, but I can't wait that long. There's only one person I can think of that would know.' Adam took out his phone and texted him:

Hi, Baz. Are you up?

Yes mate, couldn't sleep, watching a film on the box.

What's on?

Withnail and I.

Don't try the Withnail and I drinking game.

No, mate. Learned my lesson!

A work question. What does FENP mean?

Blimey, you're keen. First Edition Not Published.

Cheers!

'You've got a drink too?

Tea

Shame on you!

'What's on the front page of the one they didn't publish?' asked Ginny.

'The headline is *They Shall not Pass!* It's about the

traffic holdups on the bypass because of the roadworks,' replied Adam.

'And for the one they published?'

Liar, Liar, Pants on Fire! It's when the news broke about that politician who had denied being caught with his pants down with an intern lying to Parliament.'

'He ended up having to resign, didn't he? So I can see why they ditched the previous edition,' said Ginny.

'So where does that leave us?' asked Adam.

'One small step in the right direction. Previously, we could have guessed that the ransom notes came from within the Gazette, namely from Jason, but actually, anyone from the area could have made them. This discovery proves that they originated from within the newspaper offices because the general public never saw that first edition.

'If Jason didn't send them, have you any idea who might have?'

'Actually, my conversations with Baz and Lauren have set me thinking.' There was a pause, and then Adam and Ginny spoke at the same time.

'Dillon Richards!'

22

Monday

Adam decided it was time he uploaded some photos to his network folder. Firstly, he looked through Jason's folder to check that his own photographs measured up. *Hmm! I think his action photos of the Under-Twelves' football are better than mine. It just shows how much practice he had photographing them over the years. I think if I crop them, I can make mine more dynamic. However, I think my photographs of traffic cones at the roadworks on the bypass are far superior, much more moody, projecting an almost apocalyptic sense of gloom and despair.*

After editing his sports photos, Adam uploaded them to the network, then sat back and pondered what to do next. *I wonder if this computer system was in place when Skye was an intern.* Adam typed her name into the network folder search box, and a request for a password popped up. *So, four letters and four numbers. What would she use? The obvious thing was her name*, so he typed Skye1234. *Access denied. Maybe 4231? Access denied. I need to know when she was born - perhaps she used her date of birth like I did.* Although Adam could simply have texted Ginny and got her to ask Skye, he was curious to find what he could discover online. He could try Skye's modelling agency, and he could try Wikipedia, but first Adam tried Facebook. There it was. Adam smiled; although the date of his birthday was on Facebook, he had long since removed the year of his birth in a vain attempt to remain digitally young, without foregoing the birthday wishes that appeared annually from people he hardly knew. Adam tried the new combination. *Yay! It worked!*

One reason Adam hadn't texted Ginny for Skye's number was that he thought he could print out some of Skye's attempts at journalism to make her smile and he didn't want to spoil the surprise. What he discovered now certainly wouldn't make her happy. It was true that there were some text documents, but his screen was full of image files, and even though they were only thumbnails, he could see that they were all pictures of Skye and in most of them, she was completely naked.

One second later, he shut down his computer. One minute later, he was striding out of the building, camera in hand, wishing he hadn't seen what he had seen and on his way to take the long-distance photograph of Marcus' house for the feature on the murders.

***

Ginny had told Skye that she had work to do and had left her in the lounge chatting with her social media followers. So far, news of the murders and Skye's subsequent stay in a police cell hadn't spread. Ginny had intended to follow up on some enquiries she had received from theatre directors, but she couldn't concentrate, so instead, she settled in the lumpy armchair in her office and Tuxie promptly jumped onto her lap, demanding attention. Ginny didn't mind, though, because sitting and stroking her cat always helped her think. Adam had rung, telling her about the photos of Skye he had found on the network. She closed her eyes and gathered her thoughts.

It's another piece in the jigsaw, but it's like we are working our way around the edges and I want to get into the centre. Jason took photographs of Skye at the Gazette. The ransom notes were made there from a newspaper that never left the building. Only one sample edition was printed, and then it was shelved. Jason denied being responsible for the ransom notes when Skye met him in the woods, but that's hardly surprising. On the other hand, maybe he was telling the truth because Dillon could have found them on the network in the same way that Adam has. By all accounts, he must have been infatuated with her to have a photograph of her on his wall at home. Dillon is the piece in the middle of the puzzle that connects to the others around it. He didn't like Jason, who constantly mocked him; he had spoken to Jay in the Gazette newsroom; he perhaps felt betrayed by Skye, who had been indifferent to him, and then, when he found the compromising photographs Jason had taken of her, Dillon could have been so infuriated that he devised a plan to hurt Skye by blackmail, turning her against Jason. Also connected to Dillon was the unfortunate Marcus, who, by thwarting Dillon's career ambitions, had perhaps signed his own death warrant!

Ginny had a sudden random thought. *Here I am, trying to gather evidence surrounding these two murders when actually there were three. Just because no one seemed to like Jay except Skye - and even she had been going off him - surely he demanded some attention, too?* Ginny rang Robbie.

'Is it a good time to talk,' she asked. The sound

Robbie made indicated that he was in the Police Station and might have to choose his words carefully, but that she should go ahead.

'Robbie, I'm sure Adam has told you that I'm trying to dig deeper into everything concerned with the murders. I wonder if you could sneak out a copy of the report on Jay Prince's death?' Ginny heard a positive sound from Robbie and after a few pleasantries she said goodbye and continued with her musings.

Meanwhile, Adam was just about to take a photograph of Marcus' house when a car drew up and parked in front of the gate. *Oh, blow! That spoils the composition.* He waited as a woman in her fifties or sixties climbed out of the car, walked down the path and let herself in. *Hmm! I'll try another from the side.* As Adam pressed the shutter, the front door opened, framing the woman in his shot. What was more, she turned her head towards him. He had been caught in the act! Adam deleted the photo and walked towards the house to explain.

'I'm sorry,' he called. I didn't mean to get you in the photograph. I was trying to take a long-distance picture of the house.'

'Who are you?' she demanded.

'I'm sorry, my name is Adam Broome, and I'm a

temporary photographer for the Gazette. They, I mean we, want to do a piece about Marcus White, a very respectful article, of course.' Adam held out his hand. The lady's demeanour immediately softened and she shook his hand.

'My name is Margaret,' she said.

'I don't suppose you are Marcus White's daughter, are you?'

'Yes, I am. How would you know that?'

'My friend Ginny was a friend of your father. She used to visit him right up to the day he...he died.'

'Really? My father's nurses told me about her, but they didn't have her contact details. I would love to meet her and tell her how grateful I am for the companionship she gave my father.'

Shortly afterwards, Adam set off home, a photograph of Marcus' house in his camera and Margaret's phone number to give to Ginny. He was sure a meeting between Margaret and Ginny would help them both to come to terms with the murder of Marcus White.

23

Thursday

They had a plan. No one was very confident about it, and several were very worried about it, but still, it was a plan, and they needed one to move forward. Two evenings ago, when the group met at Ginny's house, Ginny had an idea at the back of her mind. She was reluctant to voice it. So it was with considerable relief that she heard Skye speak.

'I can't tell you how grateful I am for all your support, but also how sorry I am for putting you through all this. I feel I should be doing more, and I wondered if it might help if I met Dillon. I don't think I have even spoken to him since I came back.' Ginny's face was immediately clouded with worry.

'Oh Skye, are you sure? I must admit, I wondered if you should do that, but it could be incredibly dangerous. After all, we think Dillon is implicated in a murder. Maybe two murders.'

'Do you think Dillon knows any of the Dead Actors?' asked Adam. 'Has anyone here spoken to him?' The Dead Actors all shook their heads.

'We were all involved with the photo shoot,' said Doc, 'But we were all dressed as ordinary bystanders. I don't think any of us stood out. Personally, I only noticed him early on, and his eyes seemed to be glued to Skye.'

'That's rather an unpleasant expression, isn't it? I mean, just imagine it. Who would want a load of eyeballs stuck to them?' shuddered Julia.

'When I think of some of the things I had to surgically remove when I was in *Emergency Level Red*, I don't remember eyeballs being on my list,' mused Doc.

'What did Julia Roberts say in *Pretty Woman?* Slippery little suckers, aren't they?' laughed Angie.

'Guys, guys!' remonstrated Ginny patiently. She knew how prone the Dead Actors were to head down a conversational alley, especially if it led to a comedy club, 'Can we get back to business?'

'Sorry,' they mumbled, although they weren't really sorry. Murder is a serious business, and humour provided a welcome release.

'So,' Ginny continued, 'What you are saying is that you think that Dillon won't know you, and therefore, you could keep an eye on Skye,' Ginny continued. There were nods all round. 'Well, as it happens, as I had already been thinking about this, I have a perfect venue in mind.'

'A pub?' prompted Steve. Ginny shook her head.

'We don't know if Dillon drinks alcohol, and he might think it's a date. We don't want to raise his expectations too much.'

'What about the park,' suggested Angie, 'I could bring my dog for a walk.'

'Your chihuahua would strike fear into any murderer,' laughed Doc, 'I mean it, she could give you a nasty nip on the ankle. I don't think she could reach any higher!'

'No,' said Ginny. 'It would be harder for you all to stay close by without being noticed in the park. I think the cafe at the garden centre will be perfect. There are always lots of people milling about. You could blend in unnoticed.'

'Bagsy I sit near the cake counter,' said Steve, 'I'll pile up my plate with Victoria sponge cakes and hide behind them!'

***

Skye was ready. Everyone had arrived half an hour early to make sure they were at the best possible vantage point. Skye had picked a table in the middle of the cafe. She had dressed simply in jeans and a sweatshirt. Her phone, which was usually tucked into her back pocket, was face-down on the table - a perfectly ordinary place for it to be. Two of the Dead Actors, Steve and Julia, were already seated in the cafe. Steve, as requested, was near the cake counter, and Julia was closest to the door. Doc was sitting in his car, looking out for Dillon's arrival and in sight of Angie, who was hovering near the entrance. All four Dead Actors had little white earbuds in place, but they weren't listening to music; they were all connected to a conference call.

Ginny, was in her office and also connected to the call. 'Is everybody ready,' she asked.

'I'm ready,' said Skye. 'I'll take my earbud out when he arrives.'

'No sign of him yet,' said Doc. 'It's a shame Steve

didn't know what car he drives. Oh, hold up! He's here. He's on a bicycle!'

'He's not planning to kidnap Skye, then,' remarked Steve, 'Unless he's on a tandem!'

'Okay, quiet everybody, except Skye, of course,' said Ginny, 'We don't want to risk Dillon hearing any sounds coming from Skye's phone or her earbud. Good luck.'

A few minutes later, Dillon crept into the cafe and looked around nervously. When he caught Skye's eye, she jumped up and beckoned him over.

'Hello, Dillon,' she said, 'I was here early, so I've given my order but asked them to delay bringing it until you arrived. Have what you like and add it to my tab. It's my treat. Just tell them the table number.'

'Oh no, I shouldn't, it should be me...'

'No, no, go ahead. It's all set up. I'm having a cappuccino and a piece of Black Forest Gateau. It looks delicious.'

Dillon ordered the same as Skye and returned to the table, where he seemed lost for words. Skye smiled at him, attempting to mask her apprehension.

'It's been a long time,' Dillon said finally.

'Yes, I'm sorry I haven't been in touch before now. As you know, my life took an unexpected turn. I've been living with Ginny Fellows. Do you remember we went to interview her together?'

'I remember it very well; that was the last time you and I went to an interview together.' They paused while a waitress set down their coffee and cakes. The conversation remained stilted, with Dillon mostly concentrating on eating his gateau and sipping his coffee. Although Skye didn't feel hungry, she followed suit.

'How is life at the newspaper?' she asked eventually, as Dillon chased the last few crumbs around his plate.

'Oh, it hasn't changed a lot, but there are fewer members of staff. Regional newspapers are finding it hard to survive. I have ideas, but nobody listens, so we are sinking.'

'I meant life at the Gazette since Jason was killed.'

'Oh. Well, I still don't trust Lauren. Baz is hardly ever there - he's usually propping up a bar somewhere. Bradley acts as if he's commanding an army unit. The new guy, Adam, is a big improvement; I don't have anybody crowing in my ear about how great he is any more. Oh, I shouldn't have said that. You and Jason had a thing going, didn't you?'

'No, we didn't!' protested Skye.

'But I thought you were very happy together. Snap-happy, even.' Dillon looked away.

'It wasn't like that!' cried Skye, beginning to get angry, 'Yes, he took photographs of me, but I thought he was trying to help further my career.' There was an awkward silence before Skye reined in her emotions and spoke again. 'Dillon, if I ask you something, will you answer honestly?'

'Yes, I always answer honestly. It's what usually gets me into trouble.'

'Look at me, Dillon. Look at me,' Skye asked gently. Slowly, he turned his head and met her eye.

'Do you know anything about the letters sent to me?'

'What letters?' Skye held Dillon's gaze for several seconds while she studied his face. Could she believe him? Then, the moment was broken by the blinding white light of a battery of camera flashes.

'There she is?'

Several men with microphones approached their table.

'Skye, what do you say to reports that the murder in the woods was a quarrel between your lovers?'

'Skye, what did you do to inflame their passions?'

'Skye, Skye...'

'Oh, no,' said Steve, breaking radio silence for Ginny's benefit, 'It's the paparazzi!'

Steve jumped up, pointing to his ear to try to encourage Skye to replace her earbud, but she was too distracted and horrified to notice him. She sat mute and transfixed. Dillon dashed for the door.

'Julia, they are all men,' said Steve. 'Get Skye and take her to the ladies' toilets. I'll let you know when it's safe to leave. Doc. Are you still in your car? Be prepared to leave.'

'Okay, Steve. Shall I get closer to the entrance?' replied Doc.

'No, move further away.' Meanwhile, Julia had rushed over to Skye's table, scooped up her handbag and phone, and led her to the washroom, pursued by the reporters and photographers. Steve walked calmly over to the cash register. 'Angie, can you wait by the exit to the car park? Hang on, everyone. I'll just pay for all our cakes and coffee.'

With the bill settled, Steve told Angie what to shout and joined the throng milling outside the toilets.

'There she is, she's getting away!' yelled Angie

'She must have climbed out of the window,' roared Steve. 'Quick! This way.' Then he spoke quietly into his phone as the paparazzi rushed past him. 'Doc, when you see the reporters, start driving slowly out of the car park. Angie, let them know Skye is in the car.'

'She got in that,' shouted Angie, pointing at Doc's car. 'She's got a driver, I saw her duck down. She will be heading for the bypass.' Five minutes later, once the reporters were in hot pursuit, Angie popped into the washroom, 'It's safe to come out now. Come on, Skye, let's get you home.'

'Good work, Steve, you've passed the audition for directing this little scene. ,' said Ginny. 'Where are you, now?'

'I'm back at my table,' said Steve between mouthfuls, 'I hadn't finished my cake!'

Meanwhile on the bypass, reporters and photographers were stuck in a traffic jam at the roadworks and had now abandoned their vehicles and clustered around Doc's car. He lowered the window.

'G'day possums!' he trilled, adopting an Australian accent that gave more than a passing nod to Dame Edna Everage, 'Have you come to photograph my gladioli? They're little beauties, aren't they, my darlings!'

'Where's Skye?' demanded a reporter.

'Call me old-fashioned, but I just look up when I want to see it, darling. I do miss my Melbourne sky, though.'

As the puzzled journalists returned to their cars amidst a cacophony of blaring horns from angry, frustrated motorists annoyed at being held up, neither they nor Doc knew that gladioli were out of season.

24

Thursday

'So, where are we?' said Julia.

'The short answer is Shepton Rise,' replied Steve, reaching for his phone, 'But if you want more detail, then I could look up the longitude and latitude.'

'You know perfectly well I meant where are we with the investigation?' retorted Julia.

Ginny squeezed Skye's hand. 'I'm sorry that it got so harrowing for you in the end, Skye.'

'That's okay; I suppose I have been lucky until now,' said Skye.

'But what did you make of Dillon?' asked Ginny. 'It was hard to get a picture of what was happening just by listening.'

'It was quite hard figuring him out when I was just across the table,' replied Skye. 'All I can say is that when I asked him about the letters, he showed no sign of knowing what I was talking about. Either he has no emotions, or he hides them very well.'

'So, if we don't think that he was responsible for blackmailing you, Skye,' said Doc, 'The finger of guilt points back towards Jason, but that's not to say Dillon wasn't mixed up in the murders!'

'I wonder what Lauren did to upset him?' pondered Adam, 'Dillon said that he didn't trust her, but she's been nothing other than helpful to me.'

'Oh, I forgot to mention it. I phoned her yesterday,' said Ginny, 'I found her perfectly lovely; we reminisced about our time in the Girl Guides. She seemed just an ordinary mother with two grown-up children, a husband, a house and a mortgage, but we can't make assumptions. Who would know more about her?'

'I suppose I could meet up with Baz in a pub and see if I can get him talking,' said Adam.

'Adam, if it weren't for people like you, willing to

undertake such arduous missions, I don't know how this country would survive,' said Doc in mock seriousness. Steve promptly jumped up and, with his hand on his heart, sang the first verse of 'Land of Hope and Glory'. Angie pulled out a handkerchief and pretended to wipe away patriotic tears.

'Well, someone's got to do it!' said Adam bravely.

'By the way,' said Ginny, 'Robbie got back to me. I got in touch with him on Monday and asked if he could get me the report on Jay's death. Skye, I quite understand if you would like to leave the room for this.'

'Perhaps you could make us all a cup of tea,' suggested Steve brightly.

'No, it's alright. I'm tougher than I look. I'll stay.'

'So no tea, then,' complained Steve with a pout.

'Anyway,' continued Ginny, 'Robbie waited until all the results were in before contacting me. I had a query and he answered that this morning. These are the important bits. Firstly, Jay was shot with a .22 calibre bullet, and the rifling patterns indicate that it was fired from a pistol. That's a different weapon from the one that killed Jason and not as powerful - Jason was killed with a 9mm gun. The report said there was an entry wound but no exit wound. There was no blood on the ground where Jay was found in the woods, indicating that he was shot elsewhere. Some small traces of blood were detected inside the mask, which was one of those you get free on an aeroplane to help you sleep.'

Doc closed his eyes and declaimed: 'To die, to sleep – to sleep, perchance to dream – ay, there's the rub, for in this sleep of death, what dreams may come when we have shuffled off this mortal coil.'

'Very nice dear,' said Angie, 'I'm sure the Royal Shakespeare Company will come knocking soon.

'There's more,' continued Ginny, 'The forensics revealed one unexplained fact, but as the Police are not allocating any more funds to the investigation, they are content not to pursue it. Some red woollen fibres were trapped in the metal logo on Jay's expensive trainers. Finally, there were the photographs found in Jay's pocket. They were the extra evidence that I asked Robbie to send. I've put the printouts in an envelope, but I thought I would show them first to Skye. She might not want to share them with the rest of you.'

'My mum always said if you want a thing doing, do it yourself,' said Steve, 'I'll tell you want, Doc and I will go and make a cup of tea and leave you to it. Adam, you come too because you will know where Ginny keeps the biscuits.'

'Well said, that man,' added Doc, rising from his chair, 'It doesn't look like anyone else is going to do it. Really! You just can't get the staff these days.'

Skye opened the envelope and laid the contents on the table. She gasped in horror.

'I can see why you didn't want the press getting hold of these!' said Julia.

'It's ironic, really, because it was the local press that had them,' added Angie.

'I, I, I'm shocked!' stammered Skye, 'I've never seen these before.'

'But it is you,' said Ginny, 'And they are the same as some of the ones that Adam found on the Gazette's server. Don't worry, by the way, he only saw one of them briefly, but he forwarded them to me.'

'It's not that, it's just that I only saw them as tiny icons on Jason's computer before he deleted them. Or rather, when I thought he deleted them. So how did Jay get hold of them?' The clinking of crockery heralded the return of the men, so Skye quickly put the photographs back in the envelope.

'We decided to give you the five-star treatment,' said Steve proudly as he set down the tray, 'You have cups and saucers instead of mugs, and Adam tried to hide his favourite biscuits at the back of the cupboard, but we weren't having that, so enjoy!'

'Have you solved it yet?' asked Doc.

'Far from it,' replied Ginny sadly.

***

Later that evening, Adam and Robbie were propping up the bar in the Red Lion and chatting with the barman, Pete.

'I'll tell you what really annoys me,' said Pete. 'Fly-tipping! Can't you coppers do something about it?'

'It is annoying.' agreed Robbie, 'We get complaints all the time. It is a criminal offence under the 1990 Environmental Protection Act, but it's very hard for us to catch the offenders in the act. The worst culprits are tradesmen who are replacing someone's kitchen or bathroom on the cheap and don't want to pay for disposing of trade waste at the tip, so they just dump it when there's no one's around. Most homeowners would be horrified to know their builders were doing that.'

'There is a pile of rubbish in the lay-by at the far end of Bluebell Woods that's growing every week,' complained Pete. 'I'm often up that way walking my dog.'

'Have you told the Council?' asked Robbie.

'Well, not me personally, but I imagine someone

has,' replied Pete.

'There you go then. If everyone says that, how will the Council know to come and clear it?'

'I'll tell you what, I'll head that way when I get a chance, I'll take a photograph, and contact the Council,' said Adam.

'What a fine, upstanding, neighbourly man you are!' said Pete.

'Do I get a free pint?' asked Adam with a smile.

'On yer bike!'

25

Friday

I'm sure I can do this. It's not very far to the Corner Cafe. Margaret's text hasn't given me much time to prepare for a trip outside, but never mind. A van with a trailer full of scrap metal came clattering down the high street, startling Ginny, who had been lost in her own thoughts. *Slow down, will you? You're a danger to life and limb! That's got my heart racing. I think I should have put on a lightweight jacket. I'm really hot and sweaty. Oh, no! I know what this is. I've felt like this before. I'll have to go back. I'll just catch my breath. I need to sit down. I feel dizzy. I think I'm going to be sick.*

Ginny looked down, she coud see herself twenty feet below, sitting on a low garden wall. Her head had slumped down between her knees and her shoulders were trembling.

'Ginny.'

She wasn't really aware of what was around her.

'Mrs Fellows.'

But she could hear a voice. Where had she heard that voice before?

'Ginny Fellows.'

Ginny felt a hand on her shoulder and slowly raised her head. She saw Jackie, her gardener, looking concerned.

'Ginny. Are you alright?' asked Jackie.

'Please help me up. Help me get home.'

'Sure. I was coming to your house anyway.'

Ten minutes later, Jackie was helping Ginny to lie down on her sofa.

'Thank you so much for saving me, Jackie. Would you mind drawing the curtains and passing me my phone from my bag? As soon as I'm able, I'll have to ring Margaret White to say I can't make it.'

'If you unlock your phone, I'll do it. Just get some rest.'

'Thank you. I thought I was going to die,' Ginny whispered.

***

'What can I do for you, Adam?' asked Bradley with a smile. 'Take a seat. I don't have to ask you how you've been getting on. I've seen your work on the server. Some splendid photographs. I particularly liked those shots of the traffic cones. You've managed to make them look like Neolithic obelisks by taking them from such a low angle. Well done! I also want to congratulate you on that double spread you and Dillon put together about Skye's photoshoot. You managed to produce a piece that, despite the tragic circumstances of the day, put a very positive spin on things - the promise of youth and all that.'

'None of the photographs were mine, though. I wouldn't want you to get the wrong impression.'

'Oh, I know that. But you had to curate the piece and secure all the necessary permissions. I'll even forgive that candid photograph of me. It must have been taken moments before we heard the shot. If I had known, I would have pulled my shoulders back. It wouldn't have passed muster on the parade ground.' Adam nodded and smiled. He had often heard Baz refer to Bradley as The Major. 'Anyway, what do you want to see me about, Adam?'

'I took a series of photos today. I've printed one out to show you. I wondered if we might do a piece on fly-tipping?'

Bradley studied the photographs. They depicted a pile of broken kitchen units, cement sacks filled with rubble and broken tiles spilling out onto an old rug and topped with a generous layer of black bin bags.

'Hmm, an excellent idea, but I don't think the timing is right. I'm trying to promote a more optimistic outlook in the coming weeks. You see, I'm quite apprehensive about the future. When Marcus White's affairs are wound up, we might have some idea about who will be in control of the newspaper. Until then, we are marching on the spot.'

'I suppose if you had been in the Navy, you would have been treading water!' said Adam.

'Quite,' laughed Bradley. 'Anyway, fly-tipping is not going to go away - we can pick up on it another day. Coming back to your double spread, I've submitted it to the SMN, by the way.'

'What's the SMN?'

'Oh, I keep forgetting you are a new boy. Take that as a compliment. It's the Society of Media News. I live in hope of picking up an award. It would be good for our circulation figures.'

After he left Bradley's office, despite the shelving of his fly-tipping idea, Adam felt positive about his time at the Gazette; he was growing in confidence and ability, and it seemed to be appreciated. Like Bradley, he hoped that the future wouldn't hold any nasty surprises for the Gazette.

***

The following morning, Ginny answered the door.

'Hello. You must be Margaret, come in.'

'Are you feeling better now? Your gardener explained that you weren't feeling well and couldn't make our little rendezvous yesterday.'

'Oh, yes, thank you,' replied Ginny as she led the way to the conservatory, 'A good night's sleep made all the difference. You see, I used to keep this a secret, but lately, I've found that it helps me to share it - I suffer from panic attacks. I'm never anxious at home, so today I'm refreshed and right as rain. I used to feel guilty, but now I know it's just a condition I have to manage - although I didn't succeed in doing that very well yesterday! Do sit down, Margaret. Would you like coffee or tea?'

A little later, they were both sipping their tea - Ginny had considered having a herbal tea but decided she needed the boost that only a strong draught of builder's tea could provide.

She put down her cup, 'Anyway, that's enough about me. I want to say how upset I was that your father was taken away from us in such an untimely and brutal way. I know he was very ill, but nonetheless, it must be very hard for you.'

'I'm devastated,' replied Margaret. 'Yes, he was ill, but I was hoping we would be able to get back to the way things were. We had a big argument and hadn't spoken for years.'

'Marcus mentioned that he had written to you. I think he wanted a reconciliation.'

'Oh, that's good to know. Maybe Dad was too ill to finish his letter. I wrote to him but I didn't hear back. I should have come earlier. I was planning to come on his birthday, which would have been next week.' A tear trickled down Margaret's cheek.

Ginny nodded. 'Life has a way of catching us out when we think all is ticking along, doesn't it? There are so many things I wish I had said to my husband before he died. If there is anything I can do to help, please just say so. As long as it doesn't involve walking to a cafe on my own!'

Margaret smiled. 'I promise I won't ask you to do

that. Actually, Bradley has been a big help. When I couldn't open Dad's safe, he came round straight away, popped the contents into a box and gave me a lift to Perkins, our solicitors, for them to sort through; he's been a rock.'

'Well, as I said, just ask. Would you like another cup of tea?'

Margaret shook her head. ' I must be getting back. Thank you for being a friend to my Dad.'

26

Saturday

Although nothing had changed, and she was no nearer to solving the murder mystery, Ginny felt upbeat after her meeting with Margaret. She realised that they had each helped the other to come to terms with the situation. *I must get on with some work,* she thought, I *have a ton of emails to answer, but first, I'll double-check a few things with Skye.* Skye was watching TV in the lounge. The curtains were drawn, not so much to enhance the picture quality but more to discourage the paparazzi from creeping up to the window and trying to snap a candid photo.

'Skye. Tell me again about when you met Marcus White,' said Ginny.

'Honestly, it was only a couple of times. I hadn't given him a thought since I left the newspaper. I didn't even remember his name. One time, it was in the office. He was visiting the newspaper and Bradley introduced him to me. I can't remember what he said, but he was very gentlemanly and shook my hand. The other time was at that Gala dinner, the one you showed me the photo of with Dillon giving him evils.'

'He was what?'

'You know, looking daggers at him.'

'Oh yes. Can you explain it? What happened that night?'

'The only thing I can remember is Marcus making me change seats. I had originally sat between Dillon and Jason, but Marcus insisted that everyone should shuffle around so that I could be next to him, where Lauren had been sitting previously. He called it the seat of honour, and he made some comment about how, if someone photographed him, at least he would have a pretty girl by his side.'

'So, we can see why Dillon wouldn't like it, but I dare say Lauren didn't feel too flattered' said Ginny, thoughtfully.

Ginny returned to her office, determined to concentrate on business matters. She had emails to send out and messages to respond to. She opened one from Shakespeare's Globe Theatre. *With a false beard and a padded suit,* she thought *Steve would be perfect for the role of Sir John Falstaff. Actually, unless he spent more time at the gym and less at the Garden Centre cafe eating cake, then there would soon be no need for the padding!* Her finger was hovering over the return key, poised to select reply, when her phone rang.

'Hello, is that Mrs Fellows?'

'Yes, it is,' she replied. *Not work-related, then! No one in show business calls me Mrs Fellows. What will it be I wonder? I don't need loft insulation, new central heating, or double glazing!*

'I'm very sorry for the intrusion, but I wanted to talk to Skye Beattie. Well, actually, I would rather meet her. I believe she is staying with you.'

'Are you from the press?' demanded Ginny angrily.

'No, no, sorry, I should have introduced myself properly. My name is Karen Beale. I'm a Counsellor. Actually, I'm Dillon Richards' counsellor, which is why I wanted to speak to Skye. Dillon mentioned that Skye was staying with you, so I was doing a little detective work.' *You and me both,* thought Ginny.

'When had you got in mind?' asked Ginny.

'I'm in Shepton Rise now, so I can be at yours in fifteen minutes.'

'Would there be a problem if I sat in with Skye? She's quite vulnerable at the moment; she's been under a lot of strain.'

'That will be fine,' replied Karen.

'In that case, I will check with Skye, and unless I ring you back to cancel, we will see you in fifteen minutes.'

***

For some unknown reason, Ginny had psyched herself up and was prepared for an adversarial encounter with Karen Beale, but those feelings melted away when she met her. *Maybe I'm being ageist here,* Ginny thought, looking at the middle-aged woman sitting in her conservatory, *but she seems quite harmless.*

'I'm very sorry to be taking up your time,' said Karen, 'I'm so glad that you could both see me.' Skye gave a small, guarded smile.

Ginny came straight to the point. 'You said that it was about Dillon. I've only met him once myself when he interviewed me for the Gazette years ago, but I've heard a lot about him.'

'As I said, I'm Dillon's counsellor,' explained

Karen, 'Now, this is a rather unusual situation because, of course, my conversations with Dillon are confidential. Not only that, but also he has no idea that I have come here. I'm not too sure if I'm doing the right thing.'

'Go on,' urged Ginny, wondering if this was the moment when their prime suspect would be revealed as the murderer. Karen turned to Skye.

'I have no mandate to say this, but I want to ask if you could desist from making contact with Dillon. You see, it's not good for him. He can't cope,' continued Karen before Skye had a chance to speak, 'He has a very idealistic view of you, Skye, and he can't deal with the reality of you being back in his life.'

'I didn't realise I was back in his life,' Skye protested.

'But you sent him an email asking to meet him at the Garden Centre cafe.' Skye nodded. 'Then you are back in his life, aren't you?' said Karen.

Ginny cleared her throat. 'Can I ask, without you having to break any confidences, whether the murder in the woods has anything to do with this? Or, indeed, the murder of Marcus White in his house.'

Karen looked genuinely surprised, 'The murders? What makes you say that?'

'Well, we know that Dillon didn't care for Jason, the first victim, and he'd expressed ill feelings towards Marcus in the past. Maybe Skye's return could have triggered something.'

'No, I don't think so.'

'Then perhaps he witnessed the murders,' pressed Ginny.

'No, definitely not.'

'But what makes you so sure?' asked Ginny. 'We know he was in the vicinity an hour before Jason was shot because he appears in the background of photographs. After that, we don't know. And we have no idea where he was when Marcus was killed.'

'Well I do, I know because he was with me,' said Karen 'He had a counselling appointment at one o'clock. Neither of us, at that time, had any idea there had been a murder. In the end, he was in such a distressed state that I drove him to the City Hospital for treatment and stayed with him for most of the evening. I didn't hear about the two deaths until I listened to the news on the car radio while driving us both back. I don't think Dillon knew even then, as he had been sedated and was asleep.'

Karen Beale departed with the promise that Skye would not make any further contact with Dillon. Skye returned to the lounge to watch TV. Surprised that she could have such a profound effect on someone, she searched her mind to see if something she had said or done might have been responsible for fostering Dillon's feelings for her. Back in the conservatory, Ginny was pleased to find Tuxie in need of a lap to sit on.

'Oh, Tuxie,' she whispered as her cat purred with delight, in sharp contrast to her own mood, 'I described Skye as being vulnerable earlier, but the description is a better fit for Dillon. And it was me who instigated the meeting in the cafe which has made that poor boy's life worse.' Thirty minutes later, with her thoughts spiralling into dark, gloomy places, Ginny decided she had had enough of today. She fed Tuxie, invited Skye to raid the fridge and fend for herself, and headed upstairs for an early night.

27

Sunday

It seemed a long morning to Skye. At one point, she heard Ginny in the kitchen, but by the time Skye entered the room, the only occupant was Tuxie, who was licking her lips after polishing off her breakfast. Skye guessed that Ginny had come downstairs, fed her cat, and then returned to her bed.

Skye couldn't settle into her usual routine of watching daytime TV. The conversation with Karen played on her mind. She didn't know if she was guilty of leading

Dillon on in some way. If she had, it was unintentional, but that didn't ease her feelings of remorse. A phone call from the police punctuated her morning. After that, she returned to checking social media on her phone to see what cruel things were being said about her. She made sure she kept away from the windows at the front of the house, as a peep from behind the curtains had revealed that a few members of the press were still stationed outside.

Lunchtime arrived. *Ginny has been looking after me, but now it's my turn to look after her,* Skye thought. Skye knocked on Ginny's door, nearly upsetting the tray she was balancing as she did so.

'Ginny! Ginny! Can I come in? I've brought you a pot of tea and a cheese sandwich.' She wasn't sure how to interpret the noise Ginny made, so she went in anyway. 'Ginny, I've brought you some lunch. It's a cheese and pickle sandwich, and amazingly, I found some biscuits at the back of the cupboard. Adam and Steve must have missed them, or it would be a bag of crumbs. They look like they are from Heavenly Delights.' Ginny pulled herself up to a sitting position.

She laughed weakly, 'Biscuits that Adam and Steve didn't find! Miracles do happen. Thank you for making my lunch, Skye.'

'The police rang me earlier - they said their enquiries are all wrapped up, and I am free to leave.'

'So, when are you going?' asked Ginny.

'I'm not. That's if you don't mind me staying a while longer,' said Skye, on her way out of the room, 'Because it's not all finished yet, is it?'

Ginny began to nibble her sandwich. Gradually, she took bigger and bigger bites. Not because she was hungry, although actually, she realised that her appetite had returned, but because her mood of resignation had evolved into something stronger and more determined.

'That's right! It's not finished yet! It's nowhere near finished!'

***

Ginny didn't get out of bed immediately. She sat for a while ruminating and marshalling her thoughts. Then she reached for her phone.

'Adam, I know you were able to look at the CCTV footage, but are you able to get a copy of it to me so I can study it? Maybe you had better not email the files. Too traceable. Could you put them on a zip drive or a memory stick? I need to see the footage from the weekend Jason was killed, say from midday right through till Monday morning.'

Ginny had to get up in order to read the coroner's

report on Marcus White which was in her office. After studying it for a while, she decided to give Margaret White a ring.

'Do you, by any chance, have a copy of your father's prescription? I seem to recall seeing some copies on the bedside table along with his medicines.'

'I haven't moved anything. I'm just on my way out to see our solicitor, Perkins. I'll grab a copy of Dad's prescription and pop round with it on my way back,' replied Margaret.

Ginny went back to the source of all the trouble - the compromising photographs of Skye. They were taken before the break-in at the Gazette, which had prompted the installation of CCTV. Most of them were taken in the newsroom - not something that would happen now under the watchful gaze of the cameras. Whilst Ginny had never set foot in there, she guessed from Adam's description of the building that one set of photographs had been taken in Bradley's office. They featured Skye sitting coquettishly on the corner of Bradley's desk, swinging her legs. *How had Jay come across the photos of Skye that were found in his pocket?* she wondered.

Ginny's thoughts were swirling round and round. She thought of something she could ask Adam.

'I'm still downloading them,' protested Adam, 'These CCTV files take up a lot of room!'

'No, it's something else. This may be a random question, but is that pile of rubbish dumped in the lay-by still there?'

'No, I reported it to the council, and it's been cleared.'

'Oh. Is there any chance you can find out where it went?'

'I'll do my best!'

The doorbell rang.

'I'll go!' called Ginny, not wanting to expose Skye to any of the lurking paparazzi. Margaret stood on the doorstep, clutching an envelope. Ginny assumed that it contained the prescription that she had requested, but what was most striking was that Margaret's eyes were puffy and red. It looked like she had been crying.

'Come in, come in, Margaret,' said Ginny. 'I can offer you a cup of tea and a listening ear.'

Margaret sipped her tea, tissue in hand to catch the occasional tear that escaped down her cheek.

'Perkins warned me that, amongst the papers that I had brought in, he had found a copy of my father's most recent will. I feel I have been slapped in the face by my own Dad. Perkins said I could try and fight it, but it would be costly and unlikely to succeed. It is as though

Dad completely ignored my letter of reconciliation.'

'But what's happened?'

'To explain, I need to go back to the reason why we had the fight in the first place. You see, it was about the future of the newspaper. What Dad liked to call "the succession."'

'Your father did seem to be very proud that the newspaper had been a family business for generations,' said Ginny.

'Yes, exactly. My Dad wanted me to tell my son, Richard, to give up his job working for an oil company and come and learn the newspaper business, but I refused. I saw it as him trying to meddle and manipulate our family life. But it turned out that Richard was desperately unhappy with his job. He had been putting a brave face on it to please me. That was why I wrote to Dad, to apologise for my high-handedness and to tell him Richard was keen to come into the business after all.'

'Marcus certainly never mentioned your letter to me.'

'So when I went to see Perkins, I was expecting Dad to have left his house to me, which was the case. I was also prepared for a lump sum to have been left to Lauren, but I was surprised to learn that was not in the will.'

'To Lauren? Well, I've heard she works hard for the newspaper.'

'No, not for that reason. You see, they had a past. An affair. It was after my Mum died, but it was supposed to have been a secret because Lauren was married then.'

'I thought she was still married.'

'I believe she has since remarried. I found out about the affair, so it didn't help the relationship between Dad and me, even though he later ended it. Anyway, there wasn't any money for her. The bigger shock was that the newspaper business would be transferred to a worker's cooperative. In fact, it already has been. It was all set up.'

'That is a surprise. Marcus definitely kept that under his hat. Although we never talked politics, I didn't see him as being on that side of the political divide,' commented Ginny. *And, Lauren!* She thought to herself, *I didn't expect that either! Could could she have killed him out of revenge for breaking off the affair? Or maybe she found out somehow that she had been cut out of the will.*

28

Monday

Adam gazed at his computer screen with a furrowed brow and then reached for his phone.

'Steve, can you do me a favour, mate?'

'Sure, fire away! Oh, perhaps not the best terminology to use as we are investigating two murders. Anyway, go ahead, shoot! Oops! Go on Adam.'

'Ginny asked if I could find out what happened to that rubbish in the lay-by. I've no idea why. I'm sure if there was another dead body under it, we would have found out by now. Anyway, I'm a bit behind here at the newspaper and need to meet a deadline. I've four hundred photographs of the Under-Twelves' football match to go through and choose the best one. Any chance you could do it for me?'

'Not so good at photo editing,' laughed Steve. 'No mate, I know what you mean; I can pop down to the tip.'

'Thanks. I'll send you a photo of the rubbish.'

Steve immediately rang Julia.

'Hey, I don't suppose Rupert is at home, is he?'

'He is actually; he claims not to be feeling well and didn't go to school today. It didn't stop him from eating three pieces of toast for breakfast, though!'

'Could he knock me up a lanyard? I'm off to the council dump to check something out for Ginny. It should say something eco.'

'I'll get him to do two. I'm bored. I'll come with you.'

***

Steve inspected his lanyard.

'Excellent. TWERP, twerp: Taskforce for Waste Efficiency and Recycling Protocols. How appropriate. Let's go!' Ten minutes later, Steve and Julia, both wearing bright yellow high-viz jackets, drove into the council tip, parked beside a sign which proclaimed *No Parking*, stepped out of the car and consulted their clipboards.

'Oi!' called one of the council workers, also wearing a yellow jacket. He strode towards them, 'You can't park there!'

'As you can see,' said Steve, adopting a nasal whine and sounding completely unruffled, 'We managed to park there quite easily. We are from TWERP, and we have come to inspect your facility.'

'What?'

'We are from TWERP, and we have come to inspect your facility,' repeated Julia, speaking very slowly as if to a five-year-old. She flashed her lanyard.

'TWERP: Taskforce for Waste Efficiency and Recycling Protocols,' explained Steve.

'TWERP,' echoed Julia once more, simply because she enjoyed saying the word. 'We ensure recycling processes adhere to national sustainability standards and contribute to the UK's green goals.'

'First of all, I wonder if you know what shade of yellow your jacket is?' asked Steve.

'What? No!'

'It looks a bit like a DCY from a couple of years back,' said Steve, 'Dirty Custard Yellow.'

Julia nodded. 'It's definitely not an OBY - an Old

Banana Yellow. I'll just put down "unknown."'

'Right!' said Steve, inspecting his clipboard and looking at the photograph Adam had sent him. 'Kitchen carcasses. Where do they get recycled?'

'They go to the wood skip.'

'Your skips are made of wood? I like that!' exclaimed Julia.

'You get a tick for that, although I hope they are made from trees from sustainable forests!' added Steve, wagging a finger.

'No, the skips ain't made of wood; they are metal. It's where we put wooden stuff.'

'Oh, how disappointing,' tutted Julia, scribbling something on her clipboard. 'And what's your name, for our report?'

'It's Alf.'

'Well, lead on to the skip, Alf.'

Steve and Julia climbed the gantry next to the skip and peered down into it.

'Hmmn!' said Steve 'No sign of kitchen cabinets. In fact, there's not much in here at all. Is wood going out of fashion?'

Alf shrugged 'There may have been some last week. I don't take that much notice. It was collected on Tuesday. It will have been recycled into biomass fuel for power stations by now.'

'What about windows?' asked Steve, consulting the photo on his clipboard.

'Well, they go in our glass skip.'

'A glass skip! That's a jolly good idea!' remarked Julia. 'We will be able to see inside without climbing steps.'

'They ain't made of glass,' replied Alf, rolling his eyes.

'Shame!' frowned Julia, making a note on her clipboard.

Steve and Julia peered into the second skip.

'Of course, this is just flat glass; the bottles have their own tubs,' said Alf.

'Not a lot of glass in here, said Steve

'Full one went on Tuesday,' replied Alf. Steve took a torch from his pocket and played it over the contents of the skip.

'What have you got a torch for? It's the middle of the morning!'

'Ah! This may look like a torch. But it detects radon and methane, known as RAMA as well as the rare and lesser-known gas, Lameron. If the device finds any of those, it will emit a loud ringing noise, and we will have to run for cover. That's why we call this little beauty a Rama Lama Ding Dong.' Luckily, Alf had his back to Julia and did not see her clap her hand over her mouth to stifle her giggles. 'Lovely,' said Steve, 'That's what I call a well-kept skip. Now, what about carpets and mattresses?'

'We'll have to go over there to that covered skip,' said Alf, 'And before you ask, it ain't made of carpet.'

'Ahh!' sighed Julia. It sounded so comfy.' On peering inside, she saw one solitary, ripped mattress. 'Hmm! I don't think I will be stretching out on that!'

'Is this it?' said Steve, 'Don't tell me; the full one went on Tuesday.'

'It was Monday, actually; It will all be shredded up and made into insulation by now.'

'Well,' said Steve, consulting his clipboard. 'I think that concludes our survey. I'm pleased to say, Alf, that you should be proud of yourself, and I'm going to recommend that we install a five-star green plaque outside your entrance gates.'

Alf returned to his hut to make himself a cup of tea, feeling pretty pleased with himself. If Steve had lowered his car window, Alf would have heard his eco inspectors singing at the top of their voices as they drove away.

'We go together like rama lama lama ka dingity ding de dong.'

29

Monday

After Margaret had left, Ginny took a little time to settle. She was upset that her new friend was so distressed by the contents of her father's will, but she was also puzzled about where the new information about Lauren fitted into the scheme of things. She reached for the envelope containing Marcus White's prescription, but before she could open it, her telephone rang. It was Adam.

'Hi Ginny, two things. Firstly, I passed on the

treasure hunt to Steve, so no doubt he will get back to you with what he has found at the tip.'

'He already has, and the answer is not a lot,' replied Ginny.

'Oh, okay. Anyway, the second thing is that I plied Baz with a few drinks at the Red Lion. Guess what I found out about Lauren?'

'She had an affair with Marcus,' said Ginny.

'Oh,' replied Adam. He sounded deflated, but Ginny could tell that he had a twinkle in his eye when he added, 'Don't tell me all that drinking, telling jokes and eating peanuts was for nothing! I very nearly ate a pickled egg. I'm glad I didn't, now. Did you know she got divorced as a result of the affair?'

'I wasn't sure about the order of events.'

'Well, I can be of some use after all. Lauren confessed to her husband because she believed Marcus wanted to marry her. Her husband left her, but Marcus changed his mind. He said he couldn't, for his daughter's sake.'

'So maybe that was why Dillon said he didn't trust Lauren. He fell out with Marcus, and he knew Marcus and Lauren were in a relationship,' suggested Ginny.

'It would certainly have given Lauren a reason to harbour a grudge against Marcus, even though she later remarried,' added Adam, 'Maybe husband mark two wasn't an improvement on husband mark one!'

'Actually, I have news about Marcus' will and the future of the newspaper. Have you heard about it?'

'Bradley has called an important staff meeting after lunch. Maybe that's what's on the agenda.'

'Then I'll let him tell you all about it. I don't know any details.'

'Anyway, it's Monday. When are we resuming our film nights?'

'Oh, I've too much to think about before I can concentrate on watching a film. I want to get to the bottom of all this.'

'Well, if you can't figure it out, then no one can! It's all beyond me!'

After the phone call, Ginny finally opened the envelope containing Marcus' prescription and studied it for a few moments. *I could investigate this on the Internet, but it's not my field. It's much better to talk to a real person, and I know just who to ring.*

'Hi, Doc. I'm going to send you a list of medicines. Can you give me a quick rundown of what they are used for?' asked Ginny.

'Erm. You do know that I'm not a real doctor, don't you? After all, it was you that got me the TV part!'

'Oh, nonsense! I can't think of anyone better to ask.'

'Well, as it happens, I do have some contacts I can ask,' admitted Doc.

'See!'

***

An hour later, Doc returned Ginny's call.

'Okay. Firstly, there's Lisinopril and Losartan. They both help relax blood vessels by reducing the production of angiotensin. That's a substance that narrows blood vessels, and nobody wants that, do they?'

'No, it doesn't sound a bundle of fun.'

'The next medicine on your list is a Thiazide Diuretic. It helps remove excess salt and water from the body, reducing blood pressure. After that, he had a calcium channel blocker, Diltiazem, to help relax and widen blood vessels.'

'And the fifth one?'

That's a little more unusual. Thallium-201 is used for medical imaging when evaluating heart disease. Put simply, it helps you get a better scan.'

'I'm presuming the scanning would be carried out in a hospital?'

'Yes, that's right.'

Well, that seems to explain it, thought Ginny. *The prescription detailed four items, yet the coroner's report identified five, but he was about to go to hospital for tests, so that must be why he was given Thallium.*

***

Ginny glanced at the name displayed on her phone. It was Adam again.

'Hello, stranger,' she said.

'Here are a few names for you,' announced Adam, 'William Randolph Hearst, Joseph Pulitzer, Katherine Graham, Rupert Murdoch, and now, at the foot of the list, you find Adam Broome.'

'Really!' laughed Ginny.

'I am now, officially, a newspaperman!'

'Is this to do with the workers co-operative?'

'It certainly is. Bradley asked for a show of hands, and then all anyone who wanted in had to do was sign on the dotted line. It's a done deal!'

'Margaret was contemplating whether she should contest the will. She probably won't, but just in case, do you have someone who could look at your contract?' asked Ginny.

'Not really, I haven't needed legal advice lately,' replied Adam.

'Bring it round, I'll ask my chap to take a look. Just in case.'

'Anyway, that's not everything. I've got two more things to report!'

'Are these two things different from the ones this morning?' asked Ginny.

'Yep. Let's see if you know about these, Mrs Clairvoyant Smarty-pants. Firstly, our Youth Club won silver in the national photography competition, and one of our kids won 1st prize in one of the categories.'

'That's brilliant, Adam.'

'And secondly, you know that article that Dillon and I did together, covering the event? Well, we won a commendation from the Society of Media News. So, there's going to be a joint Award Ceremony in the Corny.'

'Isn't that technically a third thing.'

'Trust you!' laughed Adam. Ginny laughed too but then was quiet for a moment as her thoughts raced. 'Are you still there?' asked Adam.

'Yes. I'll try not to be a nuisance, but would it be okay if I came along? I presume everyone from the Gazette will be there.'

'Yes, Ginny, Of course. And don't worry, I will need to get there early anyway, so we'll have plenty of time to get settled without any pressure,' said Adam.

'I new you'd understand. Thank you. I do think I need to be there.'

30

Tuesday

I'll put the kettle on and make a drink for Skye and me, and then I really must make a start looking at those CCTV recordings, thought Ginny.

***

Lately, instead of making a mug of tea or coffee in the little kitchenette and returning to their desks, the employees at the Gazette had taken to lingering and chatting about the changes.

'Day to day, Bradley said nothing will really

change,' said Baz, 'He'll still be directing us, and we'll still be doing what he tells us to. As long as my wages appear in the bank every month, then life is sweet.'

'Aren't we getting a pay rise now that the profits are going back into the company?' asked Lauren.

'That's the trouble, there aren't a lot of profits,' said Baz, leaving the kitchenette. 'If things improve, then we'll get a Christmas bonus.'

'Oh dear!' sighed Lauren, 'Christmas! I'm not sure I can wait that long!'

'I'm the new boy, so I doubt there will be much coming my way,' commented Adam, 'But I know how you feel; life's got so expensive, hasn't it? I'm only glad I've nearly paid off my mortgage.'

'Ohh!' groaned Lauren, 'I think the phrase "a yoke around my neck" is called for.'

'The trouble is, house prices round here are high because it's so pretty,' said Adam. 'It's all very well if you're selling to move somewhere cheaper, but if you want to stay put, the increase in value is no advantage. Well, I suppose there is the temptation to borrow against the equity, which, unfortunately, is what I had to do after my wife died and I wound up my travel agency.'

'I've got a similar story to tell,' replied Lauren,'

Only in my case, it was when my first marriage ended. I wanted to stay in the family home, and, long story short, I had to buy him out of his half of the property, which meant taking out a bridging loan. Now they want the money back. I mean, what are you supposed to do when a bill lands on your mat demanding two hundred thousand pounds?'

'Ouch! Yes, behind the picturebook facade, all thatched roofs and roses round the door, lies as much trouble and strife as you'd find in an inner-city area where it's not safe to walk at night,' said Adam.

'Very poetic, Adam,' laughed Baz as he returned to swill out his mug, 'We had better start a *Thought for the Day* feature in the Gazette.'

***

Ginny was woken up by Adam's phone call.

'Oh bother!' she sighed.

'What's the matter?' asked Adam.

'I'm trying to watch the CCTV footage, and I keep dropping off, so now I don't know where I'd got up to.'

'I know. Boring, isn't it? My advice is to pause and log where you are up to at regular intervals. Then you won't have to start from the beginning again.'

'Beyond boring. Maybe I should break it up with a

yoga pose.'

'Yeah. You could do a downward dog. Oh, no; Tuxie wouldn't like that. What was that pose you tried to teach me? Mary Jane something.'

'You mean Marjaryasana, the cat pose.'

'Ah yes, Mary Jane is something quite different. Anyway, I wanted to tell you about my conversation with Lauren. I must say, I feel a bit guilty for telling tales, but as it concerns murder, I suppose I shouldn't worry. You see, she needs two hundred thousand pounds.'

***

'Shall I put your drink on the desk, or are you pretending to be a coffee table?' asked Skye, holding out a mug. Ginny collapsed to the floor laughing.

'It's Yoga - the Reverse Tabletop pose. I'm trying to awaken my mind because I keep drifting off. Staring at a CCTV screen is incredibly boring - I don't know how people do it for a living.'

'I haven't been there since I was a teenager,' said Skye, peering at the screen, which had been paused on a view of the Gazette's reception area. 'That TV on the wall wasn't there when I was an intern. Probably a good thing because I would have switched over from the news to watch a soap, and I'd never have got any work done!'

'How did you get on with Lauren?' asked Ginny, getting to her feet. 'Adam rang earlier. He said Lauren is in need of two hundred thousand pounds. Does that amount ring a bell?'

'That's how much the blackmailer asked for!' exclaimed Skye. 'I had assumed the blackmailer was a man, but I suppose there's no reason why it couldn't be a woman.'

'Well whoever it was did a very neat job cutting out the letters, so I suppose that could indicate a woman's touch,' suggested Ginny, attempting to diffuse some of the tension she could sense was building up in Skye.

'To answer your question,' said Skye, ' I don't think Lauren thought a lot of me. I remember her as being very efficient, whereas I probably came over as a wet-behind-the-ears silly girl. And she wouldn't have been far wrong. It was my naivety that got me into this mess.'

'I'll tell you what. I'll do another hour of this, then why don't we open a bottle of wine and watch a film? Something light and frothy - like this cappuccino you made me.'

'What was the name of that film where couples do

yoga on an island?' asked Skye.

'Couples Retreat? An excellent idea. I could watch that again.'

'We don't have to sit in the lotus position, do we?' asked Skye.

'No, we'll slob out on the sofa and order in a pizza. I just need to finish looking at this footage first.'

***

Okay, concentrate! Where am I up to? Oh yes. Saturday afternoon. Outside, what's happening? Nothing. One car in the car park and it's pouring with rain. Inside the newsroom. No one there. Just the TV on the far wall showing the news. I wonder why they don't turn it off when the office is empty and save some electricity? What's on? It looks like the weather forecast. Actually, I can get a better view of the TV from the camera in the reception area. Ah! Some movement. The office door is opening. This must be Karen, the part-time secretary. She's locking up for the day. It's alright for her; she's finished with the Gazette for the weekend. I've got to stay here. Switch cameras. There she goes, running to get to her car. I bet she wishes that she had brought an umbrella with her! The car park is empty now. Flick back to the Reception camera. The weather report is finished now, but they are still talking about the weather. The TV is showing a hurricane heading towards Florida. Now that's what I call rain! Time for another Yoga exercise.

Nothing is happening anywhere except on TV. It's the end of the sports roundup. A team in red have just beaten a team in blue, and the red supporters seem pretty happy about it. Ah! The screen has switched to a setting that I recognise. It's the Liver Building. So we must be in Liverpool. I'll check the other cameras and then come back to watch the news headlines.

Hmm, it's stopped raining now. That car park must have an effective drainage system. No puddles anywhere! News headlines time. Oh! It's just that politician that won the byelection being interviewed. He has a smile I don't believe, and I'm sure he will be trotting out all the things that the party leaders have told him to say. Five minutes more is all I can take, and then I'll order that pizza.

31

One week later

It was the evening of the presentation and Ginny, with Adam at her side, had arrived safely at the Corny. The Gazette had chosen one of the rooms usually used by the Amateur Dramatics Society because it had a stage. Chris Current, the local electrician and theatre group member, had positioned a microphone at the front. Adam was busy setting up a projector to show the audience a selection of the winning photographs. Meanwhile, Ginny sat quietly near the back of the room, studying her notebook. She had had a final session watching the CCTV that morning and spent a little time with Doctor Google, the friend of hypochondriacs everywhere, checking facts about medicines. Following this, she had put aside time for an hour-long yoga session, which was good for her body and, more importantly, for her mind, and then she had felt ready to venture out into the world. Skye was due to arrive later. She was on edge today, but not because of having to negotiate past the paparazzi who were still encamped outside Ginny's house, as Robbie was collecting her. She was nervous because this would be her first time speaking in public. She was to give out the awards and make a short speech at the end of the ceremony. This would be the first time Skye had ventured outside since that ill-fated meeting with Dillon in the cafe. Ginny and Skye had laughed about the situation.

'Look at us! Both stuck indoors, not daring to go out,' Ginny said, 'You had better get back out into the real world, my girl, and show them who you are as soon as you can!' Skye was determined to do just that!

Gradually, the room began to fill up, the youngsters all separating from their proud parents, to sit at the front of the room and chat excitedly with their friends. Ginny positioned herself next to the aisle so she could make a quick exit if she needed to. She noticed Margaret arrive with a young man and beckoned them to sit with her.

'Hello Ginny,' said Margaret, 'Let me introduce you to my son, Richard.'

'Actually, I think I will go and sit right at the back if you don't mind,' said Richard, shaking Ginny's hand, 'I'd rather keep to the shadows and observe.'

'I'm still not sure I should be here,' whispered Margaret, 'I still feel very raw.'

Ginny patted her hand. 'Don't worry. Trust me - it will help,' replied Ginny. 'After all, if I can get here, then it should be a doddle for you. Just promise to catch me if I faint.'

'Oh, look!' exclaimed Margaret, it's Jamila, my father's nurse.' Like the other young people, Jamila's daughter abandoned her and rushed off to join her friends. Ginny waved at the nurse and pointed to an empty seat next to Margaret.

'Hello, Margaret,' said Jamila, 'I didn't expect to see you here. And hello, Ginny, isn't it? You used to visit Mr White. I'm glad you found each other. My daughter, Tasha, took part in the competition.'

'Actually, before it all starts, do you mind if we

have a little chat about medicines?' asked Ginny.

***

The evening was going well. It was almost like being at an Oscar ceremony as the Dead Actors were the comperes and knew how to make it a fun occasion. To start with, Skye sat with Ginny because the first item was the Society of Media News award for the Cranthorpe Gazette. Bradley, pleased that the newspaper had gained recognition at last, presented certificates to Adam and Dillon. There couldn't have been two more contrasting recipients; Adam had a broad smile, amazed to be in such a position considering he was a new boy, whereas Dillon looked at the floor as if hoping the stage would open up and swallow him. Adam returned to his post next to the projector while Ava gave an outline of the photography project to the audience. Steve then invited Skye to the stage.

'You'll be fantastic, Skye,' smiled Ginny, 'Nerves are normal.' She needn't have worried. The moment that Skye started to sashay towards the stage, her modelling training kicked in; it was a confident supermodel who took to the stage. 'A star is born,' Ginny whispered to Margaret.

Now that proceedings had reached the youth

awards, the noise level ramped up and the audience cheered and clapped every photograph that Adam projected on the screen and roared their approval when anyone stepped on to the stage to collect their award.

'And now,' announced Angie, holding up a sealed envelope, 'This is the last award and the best of all. It's so secret that only Ava and Adam know whose name is in this envelope. All I know is the photographer is here in this room.' Julia stepped forward, reading from notes, although she had memorised the contents, anyway.

'The National judges said this about the next photograph. "Technically, it is flawless. It's sharp and in focus, with a beautiful canopy of dappled light framing the subject matter." However, what really engaged the judges is the way it captures the moment when nature and beauty come into contact with mankind and the potential for danger,' Julia nodded to Angie who ripped open the envelope and announced:

'The award for the best photograph in the show goes to Simon Napier, otherwise known as Snakey, for his photograph entitled Startled Deer!' It was Snakey who looked startled as his fellow club members pushed him towards the stage. Steve and Doc both dropped to their knees, bowing in homage to *Wayne's World*:

'We're not worthy, we're not worthy.'

Skye presented Snakey with a small trophy shaped like a mobile phone. For a moment, Snakey stood transfixed, then it dawned on him what he had achieved and he jumped up and down, pumping his fist, while the audience chanted his name.

Meanwhile, Baz had slipped out for a few moments. He headed to the Corny's entrance, where Charlie, the security guard, was barring the entry of the assembled members of the press. Baz stepped past him, and a few minutes later, he indicated that Charlie should let him back in. Baz was followed by two men, one holding a camera.

'It's alright, Charlie. They're with me,' said Baz.

'Blimey, it's been a long time since you were working in the Smoke, Baz,' said the man with the camera.

'Ha ha!' laughed Baz, 'Does anyone call London the Smoke anymore, Frank, what with the Clean Air Act and Congestion Charges and Emissions taxes and the like? Anyway, it's good to see you again, Frank. And you Smithy. Last I heard, you were wandering around with a Daily Mirror under your arm, acting the part of Chalky White.'

'We had to give that up. Apart from the fact most of the holidaymakers had scarpered off to Spain, as soon as anyone spotted me and claimed their fiver, they photographed me, put it on social media, and before you knew it, there were hundreds of them mobbing me. The paper was losing a fortune.'

'Now listen,' instructed Baz, 'Skye Beattie is about to close the proceedings. No shouting questions out. You'll get your interview at the end if you behave. You can take photographs, but no flash. I don't want you two spoiling things.'

244

32

Skye stepped forward. If she was nervous, it didn't show. She had given a flawless performance and was greeted with generous applause.

'There is a saying that goes, today is the first day of the rest of your life. I know because it's written on a poster in my bathroom. I've never really taken much notice until now, but, after seeing so much potential and creativity in this room, I am resolved that starting today, I shall seize the opportunity to improve on the past. It would be foolish of me to ignore the recent events here in Shepton Rise because you were all there.

Rather than forget about the past, I need to acknowledge it before I can move on. I have a confession to make. I have made mistakes, and if I had acted otherwise, people who were taken away from us might still be alive today. You see, I received a blackmail letter, and I realise now that I should have taken it to the police. I didn't, and that set in motion a sequence of events that ended in tragedy. So, I want to take this opportunity to say how truly sorry I am and to tell all of you young people to endeavour to make the right choices. And as for all you old people at the Gazette, you're probably a lost cause.' Laughter rippled through the audience. 'So to finish, I want to applaud you all - young and old and say thank you and well done.' Skye tried to make eye contact with all of the audience and clapped her hands in appreciation. She paused for a second when she saw Dillon, and he nodded. Then Skye continued. 'I honestly feel that I've been on a magic carpet ride over the last few weeks, unable to tell fact from fiction, but now I am heading in the right direction. Finally, and I appreciate that you didn't know this was coming, but I wanted to say thank you to my friend and mentor, Ginny Fellows, and ask her to say a few words.'

All the while Skye had been speaking, Frank had

been taking photographs. Only Skye, Adam, Robbie and the Dead Actors had any idea that Ginny, who had made her way down to the front, was going to stand behind the microphone. Ginny noticed that Bradley had moved to the seat that she had vacated and was chatting with Margaret. Most of the other employees were sitting in the back row along with Adam, apart from Dillon, who was way over on the far side of the room.

Ginny took a deep breath. 'I'm certain that most of you do not know who I am, but I know lots of you, if only through your wonderful photographs. Of course, I have heard about many of you at the Gazette from Adam.'

'My reputation precedes me.' Baz's announcement from the back of the room was greeted with laughter.

'I wasn't sure where to start,' continued Ginny, 'But, thank you, Skye. I will take your magic carpet idea and fly with it. I will begin by talking about a rug - a Persian rug. In its day, the Persian Empire stretched across Iran, Egypt, Turkey, and parts of Afghanistan and Pakistan. The tradition of producing hand-knotted rugs using hand-dyed yarns continues to this day. I know, in this age of laminate floors and fitted carpets, that most of you will have no idea what I am talking about, so Adam, could you show us the office picture, please? It's actually a photograph of a photograph. I know you youngsters will know how to use software to disguise the identity of the person in this photograph, but I'm afraid that's beyond me, so I cut out a piece of paper, laid it over the original, and re-photographed it. The bit of leg and the foot you can see belongs to the lovely Skye. I hasten to add that it was taken quite some time ago. And below the foot - that is a Persian rug.'

'That's our office,' gasped Lauren.

'Yes, indeed. Step outside the office door, and you will see this.' Adam was ready, and the audience saw a screen grab from the CCTV of the reception area. 'You'll have to forgive me for drifting sideways on my magic carpet because at this point I was presented with a conundrum. How do you make the rain stop?'

'If I knew that, I would be a rich man,' shouted one of the parents. Ginny joined in with the general laughter. 'See, at the top of the screen, there is the date and the time. It's five-fifty-five. Can you also see what is being broadcast on the TV?'

'It's the weather forecast. The end of our Indian Summer,' shouted someone.

'Unfortunately, you are right, Sir. If we look at the

view outside at the same time - next one, please, Adam - we can see the car park, and it's pouring with rain. Can anyone tell us what normally follows the weather forecast?' There was murmuring, but no answers were forthcoming until a parent yelled:

'The Six O'Clock News!'

'Quite right,' replied Ginny. 'So let's look at what was happening in the news that day.' This time, Adam had prepared a twenty-second clip.

'That's that shyster,' called out a parent.

'I take it you don't like politicians. I'll just show you outside again for a moment. See! Only a few minutes after the last shot, but now it's perfectly dry. No puddles anywhere. Back to the TV. Does anything strike you as odd? Bear in mind this is a Sunday.'

'Wait a minute,' shouted the previous man. The election was on a Thursday, so that creep was celebrating winning his seat on Friday. Why would they be showing it again on Sunday?'

'You've got it, Sir. They weren't. So we have a carpet ride that starts in a war-torn area of the Middle East with a young Army Officer buying a rug as a souvenir, which eventually ends up in an office in Cranthorpe. It has sentimental value because shortly after it was purchased, the young officer was injured in combat. Despite this, one Sunday he replaced the red patterned rug with a modern blue one. What is odd is that there is no CCTV record of the red rug leaving the Gazette. However, we do know where it ended up, and that's here.' Adam changed the image to his photograph of rubbish piled in a lay-by, then to another that zoomed in on the rug sticking out from a pile of kitchen units. 'So why did the rug go on this strange journey? It was because the murderer rolled up the body of Jay Gordon in it. We know because a strand of red wool from that carpet was trapped in the metal logo of the victim's trainer. This wasn't a gangland revenge killing - Jay was murdered in the Gazette's office. Once the DNA tests on that unique hand-made rug come through, it will prove that Bradley Steele murdered Jay Gordon.'

Robbie was standing in the doorway. Ginny had warned him that someone might try to make a speedy exit, so when Bradley raced towards the door, Robbie was ready. However, Robbie was used to tackling members of the general public, not men trained in unarmed combat, and before he knew it, Bradley landed a forearm smash; then, after an armlock, Robbie found himself on his back with the murderer nowhere in sight.

Robbie struggled to his feet and was confronted with a phalanx of youngsters holding their phones, videoing the scene.

'Not my greatest hour,' he groaned. Then, to those filming, he said, 'I would appreciate it if that didn't go on social media.'

'Too late,' said one.' Robbie pulled out his own phone.

'Detective Constable Robbie Broome here reporting that Bradley Steele must be apprehended. He has assaulted a police officer.'

'I know, mate,' came the reply. 'I've just seen it. It's circulating on the station chat group. Hilarious!'

'Look, you must apprehend him. He's driving a maroon Jaguar. I don't know which way he's heading.'

We are on the case; one of our patrol cars has just reported seeing a red Jag jump the traffic lights. He's heading West.'

'Whoa! He's made a mistake there. He's forgotten about the roadworks on the bypass. You'll easily catch him. Oh, nearly forgot to say - be careful. He's a murderer!'

33

Ginny sat down on the edge of the stage. There was no need for a microphone or projector any more. There was still much to discuss. The parents and young people had been allowed to return home, after all, tomorrow was a school day, and they had had enough excitement for one evening! Now everyone remaining sat in the first two rows of seats.

'Ladies and Gentlemen,' announced Doc in his best compere's voice. 'Welcome to an Evening with Ginny Fellows! Now, who wants to ask the first question?'

'Me first,' said Steve. 'So you said that the DNA tests on the rug would prove that Bradley killed Jay, but I'm amazed that you managed to find it.'

'Yes!' added Julia, 'The man at the tip told us that it would have been shredded and made into insulation by the time we spoke to him.'

'I have a confession to make. I didn't locate it. I didn't even try. I just relied on the photo Adam had taken of the fly-tipped rubbish in the lay-by and sent to the Council.'

'Ginny! How could you?' gasped Steve in mock horror.

'Well, as Sir Laurence Olivier famously said to Dustin Hoffman on the set of *Marathon Man*, "My dear boy, why don't you try acting!"' laughed Ginny. 'The truth is, I had no actual proof at all. I just knew he did it. There were a few things that didn't add up. Firstly, the pathologist's report said there were blood traces inside the mask. How did they get there? It must have been because the murderer put the mask on Jay after he had killed him. We knew from our contact in London, Cee Cee, that the murder didn't have the hallmarks of a gangland killing. Then there were the photographs of Skye in Jay's pocket. They could only have come from someone with access to the files on the computer at the

Gazette because, when Jay came to Shepton Rise, he only had one photograph. It couldn't have been Jason because he was dead, and for a while, I'm afraid, I focused on you, Dillon.' Dillon gave a weak smile in response. 'So, who else had access to the computer system? Why, the man who set it up.'

'And that's how he could switch the CCTV files!' exclaimed Lauren.

'Exactly. There was no record of him taking out the old rug on CCTV. So to go to all that effort to substitute the video, the only possible conclusion was that he had something to hide. He might have got away with it if it weren't for two things. Firstly, it rained all evening on Sunday, and yet in the film he substituted, it was dry, and secondly, he didn't notice what was on TV: news reports from the previous Friday. Again, not evidence in itself, but enough to convince me. So, it was just a case of presenting a case to you all and seeing if he broke for cover.' As if on cue, Robbie's phone pinged.

'They've got him,' he said triumphantly. 'Because they saw on the film that Bradley assaulted me, they arrested him, and apparently, he's singing like a bird.'

'Excuse me if I'm being a bit dense,' said Margaret, 'But are you saying that Bradley killed Jay in revenge, because Jay had killed Jason and my father? Why would he do that instead of going to the police?'

'It fooled me at first as well,' replied Ginny, 'You see because we all know that Bradley didn't kill Jason...'

'That's right because he was talking to me when we heard the gunshot,' said Robbie.

'...I was puzzled because I knew the photographs of Skye linked the two murders.'

'I saw a photograph on Mr Steele's pillow,' gasped Jamila, 'I didn't know why it was there.'

'Yes, the police didn't reveal that evidence to the general public because they feared they might panic if they thought that there was a serial killer on the loose. Anyway, because of the link, we assumed Jay murdered both victims.' Ginny turned towards Skye, 'And I have to say there is little doubt that Jay killed Jason. He had a gun and a motive. But it was Bradley who killed Marcus!'

'What! Why?' gasped Margaret.

'We know he was trained to kill. He saw active service in the Middle East. He once told Adam that he needed to be able to think quickly and react to a turn of events in both the army and as a newspaperman, and that's exactly what he did. Something forced his hand; he assessed the situation and acted immediately. I don't know the order in which he did this, but he lured Jay back to the office and killed him, and he suffocated poor Marcus.'

'But what forced his hand?' asked Julia.

'The reason he was in a bad mood on the day of the photoshoot and took it out on you, Lauren, was because he had learned that morning that Marcus was to be admitted to hospital for tests. Tests that would reveal that someone had been giving Marcus poison.'

'Poison! But I gave him his medicine. I never gave him more than I should,' cried a horrified Jamila.

'That's correct,' replied Ginny. 'The tablets were divided up and placed in compartmentalised boxes. You weren't to know that there were only four pills on his doctor's prescription, but five in the box. Marcus referred to them as his five-a-day. The other pills were being added to the week's supply by Bradley when he visited.'

'What was the fifth pill?' asked Jamila.

'Thallium. I've discovered that it is used in hospitals, but only under close medical supervision because it is so dangerous. Bradley was slowly poisoning Marcus.'

'But why?' asked Adam.

'To seize control of the Gazette,' replied Ginny.

'He must have been getting Marcus to sign documents when he was in no fit state to do so. Bradley wanted the new company set up whilst Marcus was still alive. I'm certain he will have destroyed the letter you wrote, Margaret, without your father even knowing it had arrived. My solicitor looked at the Workers' Cooperative contract you all signed. In reality, all the decisions and control of the finances still lie with the Executive - in other words, with Bradley Steele. I suspect it was more about power than money. Now that he could no longer gain promotion through the army, Bradley had risen as far as he could. This plan gave him the means to become the Supreme Commander. So it was he that blackmailed you, Skye, not so much for the money, although there would have been expenses setting up the new business, it was more about him flexing his muscles because he knew he could. It was a move that ultimately led to his downfall.'

'I've one more vital question,' said Steve. Ginny raised an eyebrow, thinking that she had covered everything. 'Does anybody fancy a pint in the Red Lion?'a

Epilogue

One month later

'Are we celebrating?' asked Ginny as Adam pulled a bottle of the fizz out of his bag, 'My, it's real champagne, not just Prosecco!'

'We certainly are. We signed our new contracts at the Gazette today.'

'So how has it been with Margaret's son, Richard, at the helm?'

'It's working well. Richard may not have much experience in the newspaper world, but he knows how to run a business, and he's promoted Baz to become his number two. There's not much that Baz doesn't know about running a newspaper.'

'And how does the contract compare with the last one?' asked Ginny.

'The Gazette has reverted to being a family business, as the previous contract wasn't legal, but it's now a Limited Company with the guarantee of dividends at the end of the year, based on length of service. I won't get much; I'm only too happy to have this part-time job to take my hobby up a notch, but Lauren is pretty pleased about it. She will be able to start paying off her loan.'

'How is Dillon?'

'He's doing much better. He's moved into a new role. The future of the paper is going to depend on developing the online digital platform, and that's his baby. It's going well. He's even been able to cope with seeing Skye in the building now and then.'

'Yes, I'd heard that Skye had been visiting the Gazette.'

'That's right. She and Richard have been seeing each other. They are taking things slowly, but she's been back from London a few times to see him. He took a shine to her at the awards ceremony.'

'He wasn't the only one. Did you know that I've taken Skye onto my books? A job had come up on a new Reality TV show just before that evening, and when I saw her on the stage, I knew she would be perfect. That video montage you put together for me came in handy. Anyway, I heard today she's got it!'

'Brilliant! What's the show?'

'It's called *Fantasy Castle of Love*. It was funny because when I told her about it, she said, I don't think I'm ready for any more relationships just yet, and I said, No, you ninny, it's not to be a contestant, it's to be the presenter! She won't be on her own. I can't tell you who the other compere is, all I can say is he's from a famous dance competition programme!'

'As if I couldn't keep a secret! Anyway, I'm all set to go. Let our Movie Night commence!'

'What is the film this time?'

'I thought we would move away from the photography theme to newspapers in general. I considered *Citizen Kane*, and I would love to see *All the President's Men* again, but I settled on something a little lighter, and I have *His Girl Friday* starring Cary Grant and Rosalind Russell. They make a great double act - a bit like you and me!' Adam poured champagne into Ginny's glass, and she raised it in a toast.

'Thank you and the Dead Actors, and here's to a quiet night in!' They clinked glasses. 'If we drink all this, you won't be able to drive home.' A smile spread across Adam's face. Ginny winked, 'So you will just have to walk!'

The End

A Note from the Author

Love a good mystery? Ready to dive deeper into the *Shepton Rise Murders*? Each book is a standalone story, available in paperback, ebook, and audiobook formats.

In the first book, *Murder Unscripted*, Ginny must overcome her fear of leaving the house—with support from Adam and, of course, the fun-loving Dead Actors—as she's drawn into solving the murder of one of her clients.

Murder in the Wings follows Ginny and her friends as they struggle to unravel the mystery behind a murder murder that shakes the local amateur dramatics society

This is only the start—many more mysteries lie ahead!

You can order my books from Shopify, Amazon and most online retailers by visiting: www.stuckdave.co.uk While you're there, join my mailing list for updates on upcoming releases—and a chance to win free goodies!

I would love it if you followed me on Instagram: @stuckdavewrites Finally, I would really appreciate it if you could write a review of my book on Amazon. Even if you did not buy this book yourself from Amazon, you should still be able to post a review there.

www.ingramcontent.com/pod-product-compliance
Lightning Source LLC
Chambersburg PA
CBHW031257120726
47906CB00003B/777